Dinner with The Blakemores

Olivia Gaines

Olivia Gaines

Davonshire House Publishing
PO Box 9716
Augusta, GA 30916

This book is a work of fiction. Names, characters, places and incidents are products of the author's vivid imagination or are used fictitiously. Any resemblance to actual events, locales or persons, living or dead, is entirely a coincidence.

© 2015 Olivia Gaines, Cheryl Aaron Corbin

Copy Editor: Rachel Bishop, MA
Cover: koou-graphics
Olivia Gaines Make Up and Photograph by Latasla Gardner Photography

ASIN: B010GMZQ14

ISBN-13: 978-0692479353
ISBN-10: 069247935X

Printed in the United States of America
1 2 3 4 5 6 7 10 9 8

First Davonshire House Publishing June2015

DEDICATION

For you. I wrote this one for you.

Olivia Gaines

ACKNOWLEDGMENTS

To all the fans, friends and supporters of the dream as well as the Facebook community of writers who keep me focused, inspired and moving forward.

Write On!

Est 2009

Augusta Writers

Olivia Gaines

"Easy reading is damn hard writing."

- Nathaniel Hawthorne

Olivia Gaines

Welcome to the Busy B

Well, come on inside ya'll!

Olivia Gaines

Chapter 1. Cutting it clean ...

Puente Piedra, Colombia

The early morning dew rested on the leaves of the coca plants as silent workers walked between the crops, pulling seeds from unwilling branches. Rough hands covered the tiny limbs closing over the small pods, brutally yanking off springs from the parent leaves. This field of plants is a mid-sized farm, one of the many he owns and oversees.

His morning coffee in hand, he stands on the verandah, gazing out over this arm of his empire wondering, needing, and trying to gain an understanding of how two people manage to consistently avoid his efforts to remove them from this earth. The Blakemores should have been dead two years ago. It was nearing year three and there still was no vengeance for his brother's death.

Eduardo Delgado was not a man prone to violence, but he understood all too well that some people needed to die. At the top of his list was Odessa Blakemore. A little slip of a black woman, whom he was informed had put a well-aimed bullet into the middle of his brother's head. *And for what? To save the life of Victorío Rentería?* Truth be told, he admired the man. Victorío took a shameful family business and legitimized it by selling product legally to American growers and pharmaceutical giants. In Eduardo's mind, the profit margin was smaller, but Victorío could now walk in the light.

There was also comfort in walking in the dark. In the murky part of the shadows, he could move and not be seen. This worked in his favor as many had not seen him in person in years. He was a figurehead that rarely made public appearances, which gave him the ability to live in two worlds. He, too, could walk in the light, because very few knew his face. This was something that he was counting on. He had mastered American accents and could blend in to any scenario. In a few weeks he would be heading to America, more specifically to Texas. There were some scores that needed to be settled. However, he had a few stops to make first in Mexico to handle a few disconcerted matters with Mateo Rentería. Eduardo hated getting his hands dirty, but some folks you had to kill up close.

Mateo had failed him on numerous occasions, and Saxton Blakemore being alive was at the top of his list of things Mateo unsuccessfully attempted to do. Working with others was also something Mateo failed to get done as the team had been instructed. Had he followed the plan, Hugo, his brother, would still be alive, and Eduardo would now be in charge of Rentería's estates and lucrative businesses. Mateo had miscarried his simple portion of the planned task. For this and many other reasons, he liked Mateo even less than he liked his overly ambitious brother. Yet family was family and unfortunately, a person could not choose who they were related to by blood.

It was still unclear to him what made Hugo make a move a week earlier than they had planned. Eduardo was still solidifying alliances in Colombia when his brother made his play. It was three days from his due arrival in Mexico when he received word his brother, Hugo had been killed. What was really odd was that the woman was a fluke – an unknown variable that showed up out of nowhere. Mateo, always one for playing sadistic games, pulled Odessa Blakemore into the takeover scenario. Stories were sketchy on how the women sex workers were freed from the holding pens, or how the inventory was spared, and everyone got away scot-free with the exception of his brother. It all gave him a headache.

Eduardo squinted his eyes as he watched the Jeep bumping over ruts on the dirt pathway as it made a beeline to where he stood. A vehicle moving at that speed was never the bearer of a good word. Today, he was not in the mood to hear one more word of bad news.

"Señor," Mariana, his assistant and right hand called to him. "I am told that Mateo Rentería is in that approaching vehicle."

"Well, my morning just became interesting," Eduardo said to the lady. He handed her his cup for a refresher on his coffee.

He had not moved from the banister that supported his weight. At 175 pounds of lean muscle, Eduardo was an attractive man. Unlike his brother, he had been educated and attended university in Colombia, achieving a degree in agriculture. He knew the fields. He knew how to touch the land and make it productive. If it were barren, with a single touch of his hand life would grow. He never abused the soil, nor the workers who overturned the fertile valleys so they, like he, could continue to eat. It was well known that he was a fair man but he was also a planner. There were very few things he did by the seat of his pants. Everything was well thought out. Even as he moved forward with his ideas to take over Rentería's businesses, Mateo was his backup plan. His long-term plan was far more nefarious.

He watched the Jeep roll along, coming through the main gate of the hacienda, rounding the curb and kicking up far more dust than was required. "It is hot this morning," he said to Mariana as she handed him a fresh cup of his fine Colombian roasted coffee.

The car came to a screeching stop as Mateo jumped out of the black utility vehicle, still carrying that silly golden handled machete. Eduardo never like gimmicks. Either you were a bad guy or not. There was never a reason to taunt people you were going to kill.

Mateo was grinning at him. "*Buen Dia*, Señor Delgado." He was beaming from ear to ear as if he had good news to bring him.

He did not. The last few trips to his home, the machete wielding henchman had not brought any news that was good nor of any use to him. Eduardo saw no reason for the man to open his mouth. Slowly, he handed his coffee cup back to Mariana as he pulled a loaded 9mm from the back of his waistband, pointed it at Mateo's head, and fired. The insipid smile was permanently frozen on his face.

Using his silver tipped boot, he pushed the body off the porch onto the ground. The machete lay askew on the stairs, the sun glinting on the gold handle and silver blade, shining a fresh idea into Eduardo's face. With care, ease, and minimal effort, he picked up the machete to test the balance of the blade to the handle. "You know, this is nice. I see why he liked it so much," Eduardo said. He wanted to test the sharpness.

Raising the blade high, he came down with full force, severing Mateo's head cleanly from his body. "Hmm, it is sharp, too," Eduardo said with downturned lips.

He eyed Mateo's lifeless form on the ground at his feet.

A simple request was made of the man: kill the Blakemores. Instead, he received reports of Victorío on a cruise ship in a conga line. It was even more insulting to get the report that a friendship had developed between the Blakemores and Victorío. It was all so tiresome; it was a simple job that could not seem to get done to his satisfaction. Eduardo had an inside man. His inside guy was doing a far better job than he had hoped giving him vision into the daily lives of Saxton and Odessa.

Eduardo pointed to the head on the ground. "Mariana, please put that on dry ice with coffee beans before boxing it up and sending it to Victorío Rentería," Eduardo said as he took his coffee from her hand.

"Is there a note to accompany the head?" she asked him.

"No. The head is message enough," he responded. He stepped over the body to take a walk to the stables. It was a good morning to go for a ride.

After the ride he would call Corpus Christie.

Chapter 2. A stranger in the house ...

Corpus Christie, TX

Ryanne Trodat Dobbins awoke with a start. Her heart was racing, but as she tried to sit up in the bed, a heavy weight held her down. Fear and Uncertainty sat on her chest like a set of twins forbidding her to move. Her arm slid out to check the other side of the bed for her husband, Dwight; he wasn't there. Her ears strained to listen for what she could feel was wrong in the air. The mood of the space in which she resided felt thick. Dense. Goosebumps formed on her arm as she grabbed a hold of Fear and pushed it off her chest. Uncertainty was holding her in the bed as she heard her husband's voice speaking low. *Is someone in our house?* The inner dialogue that was playing in her head was at war with her reasoning as one cautioned her to stay in the bed while the other forced her legs to swing to the side and propel her body from the mattress. Common sense held her hand as she bent to get on her hands and knees and retrieve the Ruger .380 automatic from under the side of the bed.

Her father had always taught her to keep one in the nightstand and one under the bed out of plain sight. "Pumpkin, if you have to hide under your bed, you will never be alone," Big Sarge had told her. His advice tonight was probably going to save her life. She slipped on her robe and dropped the piece into the right pocket.

The clock on the nightstand glowed with red numbers telling her it was only 3:30 in the morning. *Who is he talking to at this time of the morning? We don't have State Farm and I know that is not Jake.* Dwight's voice was low as he spoke into the cell phone. Caution held her leg as she came to the corner of the kitchen where he stood by the sink. The light from the stove hood was the only illumination in the room, casting an eerie glow on the side of her husband's face.

"She's sleeping. It's the only time I get a break from that chatting mouth of hers," he said low into the phone.

Ryanne blinked several times as her brain absorbed his words. *Don't let him know you are here. Listen. Learn.*

"Yeah, I should be paid extra for having to sleep with her. She is a dead fish in bed and it matches her personality. ... No she is nothing like her sister, Odessa, that one, I would make love to for free," Dwight said in the line.

It was as if the air had been sucked from the room and Ryanne found herself getting light headed. Yet she was rooted to her spot. Still listening to her husband.

"Not really much else to report. Odessa is about six months along in her pregnancy. We are scheduled to go to Dallas for Thanksgiving and I will once again be forced to be in their company," he said to the person on the other end.

"Saxton ... right now he is pretty happy about becoming a father. I think it would be poetic to poison him over dinner because Odessa can't cook worth a shit. Letting her live with the guilt that her cooking killed her husband would probably destroy her," he answered the unheard voice on the other end.

The room was quiet as she watched her husband standing there, taking instructions from an unknown voice in the middle of the night. "Yes, Señor." Dwight responded. There was a lull in the conversation before her spouse responded, "It depends on how fast you want to move. I could go into the bedroom and put a bullet in her head and call it a night, or do you want to wait until they are all together in a couple of weeks and come in and handle it yourself?"

The tears had started to roll down Ryanne's cheeks. Her husband was worse than a cheater, he was ... he was ... he was standing in front of her.

In the dimly lit room she was grateful she could not see his face. She hated him. He was a liar. He had lied to her. Their whole marriage was a lie. He was a stranger in her house, in her bed, and in her life.

"How much of that did you hear, my wife?" he asked as he stood close. His breath caressing her cheek like an unwanted lover.

"I just came downstairs to get some water," she lied.

Dwight took his hand and pressed it into her shoulder, pinning her against the wall. "And the idea of getting water made you cry, Ryanne?"

Her throat was cracking. "Yes. I am really thirsty."

The man she was married to, as she refused to call him her husband any longer, threw back his head and actually laughed at her. "Wow! All those book smarts and not an ounce of common sense. I sometimes have wondered how you have managed to feed yourself and walk at the same time," Dwight said to her. He used his left hand to flip open her robe. A long index finger trailed down the front of the nightgown, his hand resting on her breast. "Damn shame, really. I was actually starting to warm up to sleeping with you. You were progressing nicely, learning how to please me."

There was more of Dora Trodat in her than the man

realized as her knee came up fast and hard to his groin. Dwight doubled over as Ryanne started to run. She didn't know where or which way to go. She could not make it to her car. Her feet were bare and she was only wearing a nightgown and robe. The moment of indecision was all he needed to regroup as he caught her in the hallway, tripping her up and landing heavily atop her. The air was nearly knocked from her lungs as he crawled over her. She could feel his excitement against her thigh as he pushed her gown up and groped at her underwear.

"One last ride before I kill you sweetheart," he told her as he ripped away her underpants.

Ryanne's hands went up and scratched at his face, trying to gouge out his eyes. This was the turning point in the whole frightful affair, when Dwight Darrel Dobbins raised his hand and smacked her hard across the face. The sweet, unassuming woman that he had been married to for six months changed before his eyes. The fear that he had seen in the kitchen was gone and a very angry bitch was staring him in the face.

"You hit me?" she asked. For a second, Dwight felt fear. Ryanne repeated herself but this time she said it as a fact. "You hit me."

Her knees came up and dumped him on the floor next to her as she popped to her feet, kicked him in the chest and lowered herself into a karate stance and socked him in the life givers. "My daddy ain't never laid a hand on me and neither will you, you piece of ..."

Dwight, groaning loudly, grabbed her ankle and flipped her back to the floor. Ryanne scrambled to get back to her feet as she made a beeline for the bedroom. *He knows where my gun is. I have to get there before him.*

He was on his hands and knees, but he was moving quickly down the hall, trying to get to the bedroom before she got to that gun. She burst through the door, stumbling, falling, rolling across the floor, but he was bent at the knee as he dove across the bed and reached into the nightstand, pulling out the weapon. She had not been fast enough.

"Now, where were we?" he asked as he patted the mattress for her to come and join him on the bed.

The clip was loaded in the weapon but Dwight didn't know the first round was a rubber bullet. Saxton had taught her that trick. Even if he fired, he would only slow her, and not kill her. She bolted for the door.

"Shit!" he said as he jumped off the bed to run after her. She almost made it out the front door when a heavy hand hit her again upside her head, sending her careening across the floor. "Stop being so difficult, Ryanne," Dwight said to her.

He moved like a panther coming towards her. The man was taking pride in watching his wife scramble backwards on the floor to get away from him. It was probably a wise thing on her part considering what he was about to do to her. "Now, come to Daddy, and let's get this over with it."

Her face was without emotion as she pulled the .380 out her pocket. "You ain't my damn daddy!" She was sliding backwards as she pulled the trigger three times. One shot went wild and lodged into the ceiling as he ducked low, still charging at her. The second shot wedged in the door as he grabbed at her leg, trying to pull her close enough to get the gun from her hand. The last shot landed in flesh as Dwight collapsed on the floor.

Chapter 3. A cry in the darkness ...

Dallas, TX

The burgeoning rays of a new morning penetrated over the horizon and peeked into the window of the Blakemore home signaling Saxton's body that it was time to rise. It would be nearly an hour before his wife, Odessa, would awaken, but a kicking fetus had its own hours. When dawn broke through the darkness, slapping at night's oppressing hand, it too wanted others to awaken. It appeared that someone else desired the same thing.

Saxton's phone vibrated on the nightstand. Almost in stealth mode, he grabbed at the spot where he thought he had laid the black item, which was on the corner of a dark table in a near pitch-black room. *Grab it before it wakes her*. Odessa had slept little in the past two weeks because no matter how hard she tried, either her mind or their son would not let her rest. Initially, they had believed she would be having twins, but it turned out the second heartbeat was only gas. She still had nearly three months to go before the pregnancy came full term, but the way the little fella was carrying on, you would have thought he was with his grandmother Dora at a towel sale.

The phone buzzed again as he located the mini idiot box and slipped out of bed. In the bathroom he slid his finger across the screen and jammed the phone to his right ear.

"Blakemore," he said in a hushed tone.

The voice on the other end was muffled through the sound of tears. Saxton pulled the phone away from his ear to look at the caller information. It was Ryanne.

"Ryanne, are you okay?" Fear flooded his heart as he had a flashback to getting a similar call many years ago from his sister. A call from Belva that also came in the wee hours of the morning. A cry in the darkness for help.... He changed his tactics and chose his next words carefully.

"Are you in immediate danger?"

The sobbing voice mumbled, "No."

"Are you hurt, Ryanne?" He wanted to know. Yes and no answers were easy, even to a person entering into the early stages of shock.

"I'm not hurt, but he is...."

Saxton inhaled deeply, his mind slapping about ideas, scenarios, answers, and *what ifs* as he thought about flight times. It would take his brother, Connard, at least an hour and a half to get the plane to Dallas. The flight from Dallas to Corpus Christie was another hour and some odd minutes. It would take the police that long to stop scratching their asses.

The next question was critical. "Ryanne, is Dwight dead?"

More sobs. A gasp of air. "No ..." she mumbled into the phone. "He is bleeding a lot...."

Saxton the big brother went into overdrive like he had when Belva had called him years ago with a similar plight. He spoke slowly. "When you hang up, take the chip out of the phone and crush it. Call 911 from the house phone and try to stop the bleeding. Do not open your mouth when the police arrive and pretend like you are in shock. Do not say a word until we get there. We'll be there in three or four hours."

She was still sobbing. Saxton's tone was firm. "Ryanne, repeat what I just told you."

Odessa was standing in the doorway listening to his voice as her sister mumbled back the words in the phone.

"Ryanne, three hours, we will be there in four hours max," he told her.

The muted rays of November light broke through the curtains in the bedroom, shining fresh new light into the room and the current situation. Odessa was scrambling to find a pair of pants, shoes, and throw some water on her face. Saxton was calling his brother.

"Connard, I need the plane sent to Dallas with a continuing flight on to Corpus Christie. Four going out, five returning," he told his very groggy little brother. Connard did not ask any questions as he could count on two fingers the number of times Saxton had requested the use of his private plane.

As he dressed he asked Odessa, "Have you awakened your parents? They need to be dressed with full bellies and ready to go in 45 minutes." He looked at her stomach. "The same goes for you two. Food, water, snacks in a bag. We have wheels up in less than two hours."

Odessa wanted to ask questions, but if Saxton was calling for the plane, it had to be bad. How bad, she didn't know and she wasn't sure she wanted to know. However, in her condition, surprises were not welcomed.

Curiosity and fear for her sister pushed her to ask the question, "Saxton, is Dwight dead?"

"Not to my knowledge," he responded to his wife. He gave the same response again fifteen minutes later after he spoke with his friend and lead agent in the CIA, Marecus Roget.

"What do you need from me, Blakemore?" Agent Roget

asked into the line.

Saxton understood how the justice system worked. The more money you had the better lawyer you could afford. The better lawyer you could afford, the less likely your chances were of ending up in a dark cell fighting off predators in the wee hours of the morning. Dark cells filled with greedy predators who intentionally sought to abuse and destroy your self-esteem, reducing the strongest being to a pile of nothing.

"I need the best defense lawyer you can get for me in Corpus Christie. I need them up, dressed and headed over to the house to meet Ryanne," he told him before swallowing a cup of decaf, gnawing into a whole wheat bagel with reduced fat cream cheese, as he stuck the keys into the ignition, turned over the engine, and backed out of the driveway. Odessa was riding shotgun and holding on to the *oh shit* bar as he yanked at the gearshift, putting the truck into drive and heading towards her parents' home. He slowed the truck for a minute and placed his hand over her belly. His son was awake and moving about. "Everything is going to be okay," he said to his wife and it also calmed the child.

After only two years and six months of marriage, Odessa's parents, Big Sarge and Dora Trodat, understood the type of man their daughter, Odessa, had married. Saxton Blakemore was a stand up type of man who fought for the little person and enjoyed taking out the bad guy. Their eldest daughter, Ryanne, they were certain, had married everything that Saxton Blakemore was against. A bad guy pretending to be a loving husband. As much as they wanted to scream at the top of their lungs that something wasn't right about Dwight, time, patience, and the choices of their children were things over which they had no control.

Only six months into the marriage and they all dreaded the worse – that Ryanne had killed her husband; something each member in the family feared would happen. It really wouldn't be that big of a shocker because changes in Ryanne's behavior became noticeable after only two months of marriage. Her phone calls became fewer. Face time ceased after Dora commented on how haggard she was looking. The fire that used to be in her eyes was a dull gaze. Four months into the marriage, a concerned Odessa traveled to Corpus Christie to spend a weekend with her big sister, but had to leave early. It was too uncomfortable for everyone involved. Ryanne was on pins and needles and Dwight was rolling up the welcome mat.

"She's my sister and I will visit any damn time I feel like it, Dwight," she told him and sat firmly in the chair. Even pregnant, Odessa dared him to make a move towards her. She knew the man was a cunning snake, but Big Sarge had taught his daughters well.

No man was going to rule them, least of all a weak one like Dwight.

Olivia Gaines

Chapter 4. Buckle up ...

There were so many changes and challenges occurring with Odessa's family. As Big Sarge secured the front door, she watched her father's movements, which had begun to get slower over the past few months as the pain in his right hip increased. Her mother, however, had not lost a step. It still confounded her to no end how the woman had an outfit for every occasion.

Dora was dressed smartly in camouflaged pants, black boots, and a black pea coat. The true eye catcher was the scarf she wore around her neck. Before she could comment on it, Dora slid into the backseat of the truck, pelting Saxton with a million questions.

"Saxton, what has happened? Is my baby okay? Did she shoot Dwight?" Dora asked.

Big Sarge was struggling to climb up into the truck as Saxton's eyes went to the rearview mirror. On the steering wheel he pressed a button, and an extra step lowered from the running board, giving Big Sarge some additional footing to climb up and prop his good hip on the seat. Odessa's hand went to her husband's arm. "So that's what that button does."

Saxton winked at her as Dora turned to her husband, grabbed him by the back of the coat, and pulled hard. Big Sarge landed on his back in the seat, his face almost in Dora's lap, as she looked down at her husband. "Would you stop playing around, man, our baby may be in jail! Saxton, is she in jail?"

"We don't know that, Ms. Dora," he told her.

"Well, did she kill the bastard?" Dora implored.

"I have no knowledge of the status of Dwight," Saxton told her as he kept his eye on Big Sarge, waiting for the rear truck door to close.

Dora was trying to remain cool. "Has she been arrested, Saxton?" she asked, her voice rising an octave.

Big Sarge was secured in the seat as Saxton put the big Ford into gear. "I am not aware if she has been arrested."

He remained cool as his mother-in-law formed a face he had never seen before on the woman. Dora's brow was furrowed, her mouth was tight, and she stared him down through his rearview mirror. "Well, what the hell do you know, Saxton?"

Saxton mumbled under his breath, "Now I know why Ryanne called me." Odessa rubbed at his arm, while her other hand rubbed her belly trying to calm his son that was either turning in her womb or playing soccer.

Big Sarge was doing his best to calm his wife. "Dora, compose yourself. I am certain that when she called Saxton, he made some calls and she is going to be okay until we get there." He patted his wife's hand as he made eye contact with Saxton through the rearview mirror. Saxton nodded his head in agreement. Understandably, he too was worried and Dora wanted more details.

Saxton had none. She opened her mouth to say something that Big Sarge was certain would make Saxton want to climb in the backseat and throttle the woman, so he held his wife's hand. "Dora, she will be safe until we get there."

With his other hand, Big Sarge reached along the side of the seat to nudge Odessa's arm. She picked up on his cue and turned in her seat, as much as she could with a small watermelon-sized belly restricting her movements. "Mom, that is an interesting scarf," she said. This of course changed the subject a bit. "Are those little dots on it?"

Dora used one hand to free the scarf from her neck so she could take a closer look at it. "No, those are Army ants."

"You have a scarf with Army ants on it ..." Odessa said and then she thought about where it could have come from and she got quiet. Her mother would do the rest.

"Mary Jean sent me this for my birthday last month. It is rather warm and of course it matched my outfit," Dora said with pride.

Saxton's eyes went to the rearview and looked at his in-laws in the backseat. They were exceptionally loving people and even better parents. Some Saturdays, Saxton felt guilty for enjoying his fishing time alone with his father-in-law, because he could not remember the last time he had fished with his own father. As he drove to the airstrip, his eyes would periodically glance into the rearview mirror as Odessa soothed and occupied her mother by talking fashion. A pang shot through him as he got a flash of a memory of his mom helping him pick out a tie for Easter morning service for church. *When this is all settled, I am going to head home for a few days.*

"That's nice, Saxton. But it would be nicer if you could tell us where we are heading now. You missed both exits to the airport," Dora said loudly.

He had not realized he'd spoken the words aloud. Then Big Sarge wanted to know the same thing as Saxton turned the truck down a dark road entering a landing field that seemed to be in the middle of nowhere. "Saxton, son, where are we going?"

The crow's feet around his eyes crinkled as he smiled into the rearview at Big Sarge. "We are going to meet our ride."

Odessa remained cool as the truck bumped along an unevenly paved road. Big Sarge's mind was in overdrive. "Who are we meeting in a back field, some drug dealers?" A wayward thought struck him as he grabbed the back of Odessa's seat and leaned forward. "Awww, hell naw! Are we using your Mexican drug dealer friend's plane?"

"His name was Rentería, honey," Dora chimed in.

Big Sarge wasn't hearing any of it. "I don't care if his name is Pancho Villa. What if we get shot down flying over US airspace?"

"Daddy, stop overreacting," Odessa said softly.

"I don't care if he borrowed the plane from Kay Zee, as long as we get to my baby," Dora said with an uncharacteristic neck roll.

Saxton chuckled, giving his wife a sideways glance, "Odessa is she trying to say Jay Z?"

Odessa stared out the window as if she didn't hear any of them. In the distance, the bright lights of the runway seemed to be cranked up. In the early sun of the morning, the lights of a plane could be seen as Saxton maneuvered the pick up to a small office. In less than five minutes the plane was on the ground and turning. It did not escape anyone's notice that the side of the plane read Blakemore Oil.

"Saxton? You have your own plane?" Dora asked with her eyes wide.

He shook his head as he opened his door, then his mother-in-law's to help her out of the vehicle. "No, ma'am, it's my brother's plane."

Big Sarge was mumbling as he opened his door and watched Saxton walk around the truck to assist Odessa. "You mean to tell me I bought all those commercial tickets to Puerto Rico when we could have been flying all high class like Kay Zee?" Big Sarge said.

"Daddy, we flew commercial to Puerto Rico as well. This is a favor Saxton called in for us ... for Ryanne," Odessa said as she took her husband's hand.

The past hour and a half flew by so fast that the plane was not really the main issue; not knowing is what was bubbling to the surface. As close as the Trodats were to Saxton, this was a part of his life that he never spoke about. The plane proved it and raised more questions; none of which he was ready to discuss or answer.

The stewardess opened the door to welcome them aboard the plane. The carpeting held the Blakemore logo with the oil rig in the center. The leather seats of the plane were embossed with the same logo; so was the stewardess outfit. The whole scene reeked of Blakemore money and pride. Saxton seemed uncomfortable with all of it. The pilot came across the loudspeaker to offer an early morning greeting as the plane taxied and was back in the air. "We are airborne to Corpus Christie. Our flight time is a little over an hour. Jeanine is back there to make you breakfast, get you coffee, and make sure you folks are comfortable during the flight."

Big Sarge shifted in the seat but his eyes remained focused on his son-in-law. "At some point, Saxton, when you are ready, I would like to know why you gave all of this up."

Saxton's hand was interlaced with Odessa's as he leaned back in the seat and closed his eyes. Over the years he had given up a lot. He, too, knew it was time to reclaim a great deal of it, not just for himself, but also for his son.

Chapter 5. Broken toes and broken spirits ...

Puente Piedra, Colombia

When the call came in, Mariana wanted to turn the phone off and pretend she had not heard it ring. This was not good news. Further, it was going to put her boss in a really bad mood for the remainder of the day. Yet he needed to know.

Eduardo was not a man prone to violence. In truth, it brought him more pleasure to be in his fields, checking his crops and caring for his workers. However, he liked power. He wanted a great deal of it, but he never could seem to get there. Each two steps he gained, he was knocked back four. Of the four Delgado brothers, only two were still alive, and Eduardo was without question the smartest of the lot.

Hugo, the eldest, a soldier for hire, was the one who craved power like an addict for chocolate. Each day, each minute of his life, he aligned himself with powerful men, waiting for an opportunity to take over their lives and steal what they had earned. Andres, the second oldest, was a fool. He supervised the production facilities for the farms that harvested the coffee and the coca. For some damned reason, Andres decided he knew a better method to extract the cocaine from the coca leaves. It is a delicate process of balancing the acids and solvents, but to test the product on himself was foolish. He was found in the production house with a grotesque smile on his face. Under Eduardo's direction, Andres was given a closed casket funeral. Their mother did not need to remember her son in that way.

Eduardo was the third son. The keeper of the name. The carrier of the line. The father of the four children he was training to take over the family business. However, the business was not nearly enough to put four children through school and he needed to branch out. Initially, he had no qualms with Rentería, and he respected the man, until he decided to go legit. This cut Eduardo's income by a fourth. It was a fourth too little. There were many branches in his business; he could not allow a single leaf to hit the ground without directing its path. Rentería had ventured from the footpath. Worse than venturing off, he didn't take anyone with him on the new journey. This is what truly irritated Eduardo.

Mariana joined him on the lanai as he read through a periodical on harvesting techniques. He looked up when she walked out. "You know, Mariana, it is a sad day when you cannot even trust the bad guy to stay bad."

She froze in her steps. Eduardo knew she had a bad update. "Don't be shy, my dear, tell me more information that is going to ruin my day."

She was trying to remain strong as she delivered the news. "Dwight Dobbins has been shot. He is in Mercy General in Corpus Christie. I do not know, Señor, if he is going to make it."

Eduardo rose slowly from the seat. He inhaled deeply and exhaled with purpose. These were the times which frightened Mariana the most, when he seemed very calm.

"Who put the bullet in him?"

Mariana stepped back before delivering the news. "His wife."

The silver tipped boot came up and out with force as he kicked the wood post that held up the roof. It hurt his too as he balanced on one foot, hopping about the patio, swearing like a sailor in a whorehouse. *"Ay Dios Mio!*

What does it take to kill those damned people?"

He flopped down in the chair, raising his leg to rest on the footstool. The fight seemed to have left him. Mariana spoke softly. "Is there anything I can do for you, Señor?"

His fingers were over his eyes, rubbing softly, trying to hold back the pain. "*Sí, por favor*. Please call *el doctor*. I think I have broken my toe."

Corpus Christie, TX

Ryanne watched the mouthpiece that Saxton had hired to speak with the police as she sat clutching her purse. *Great, I grabbed my purse with my phone but didn't put on any panties.* Photos were taken of her face, the side of her head, her ankles, and the bruises to her back where she had fallen on the floor in her attempts to escape Dwight's assault. What she could not escape were his words. Mean words. Nasty words. Ugly words that kept coming at her face like hard blows crushing the bones that supported her smile. *I thought he loved me. All of that. All of it was to get to my sister?*

A ruckus was taking place in the lobby and she knew her parents had arrived. She checked the clock on the wall. 8:15. Four hours. Just like he promised. Saxton had brought the cavalry, but for Ryanne, it was too late. The herd was already out of the fence and her faith had been rustled by sidewinder that had sunk his fangs deep into her psyche. She had known better than to kill him, but there would be several things he would never be able to do again.

At the top of that list was hurt another woman; following in a close second was the ability to be a father. Dwight was physically broken but so were her spirits.

Odessa walked through the door first. Her rounded belly pointing at Ryanne, reminding her of something else she was not going to have with her husband. She was only older than Odessa by a year, but her sister was more like their father. She had a quick wit and an outgoing personality. Everyone who met her instantly liked her and men all wanted to be with her. It wasn't as if she was the prettiest girl in the room. She was just always in the damned room. Filling it up with her *Odessaness*.

It wasn't as if she was jealous of her sister, but secretly, she coveted her confidence. There was no doubt that Ryanne was the smartest of the three children. She was proud of the two master's degrees she had earned, as well as a doctorate in finance, but relationships had never been her thing. When Dwight came on so strong, then asked for her hand in marriage, Ryanne was overjoyed. She was going to be married, have a family, a career, and be happy. *Happy*. Right now, she was happy she had put a bullet in him.

Her parents burst through the door, startling the large lawyer.

"Baby, what happened?" Dora implored.

"Are you alright, Pumkin'?" Big Sarge wanted to know.

Odessa only held her sister's hand as Saxton stood in the corner watching the family rally around his crumpled sister-in-law. The bruises on her face took him back to a memory that he often tried to forget.

"Oh my God, look at her face," Dora was crying as she pulled her child into her bosom, trying to rock away the pain. Ryanne's eyes were glazed and trying to connect to her family.

"What do you need, Pumkin?" Big Sarge asked.

Through dry lips and a quivering tongue, the only words that Ryanne uttered since calling 911 were spoken now. "Take me home, Daddy."

Big Sarge leaned in to whisper in Ryanne's ear, "Sure thing, sweetie, but I have to know, did you kill that mutherf-..."

Odessa called to him, "Daddy!"

He wasn't hearing it. "Aww hell! Y'all wanted to know, too, but just didn't want to ask. Saxton, all over in the corner with that plausible deniability shit. I want to know did she kill that rotten mutherf-..."

"Daddy!" Odessa called again.

Big Sarge was muttering under his breath, "I'm just saying, 'Dessa. You gonna pull the trigger, you need to drop him like a sack of shit ... that low down, conniving mutherf-..."

"Daddy, please. She is upset and traumatized. You are not helping," Odessa implored.

Saxton was speaking with the attorney, making sure they would be able to take her home. Bertha Stollings handed her business card to every member of the family. "Just make sure when she comes back to get her belongings and anything else from that house, you call me first."

Saxton handed her a business card for Blakemore Imports and Collectibles. "Will do. Make sure you send the bill to this address and I will take care of it."

Ryanne, still clad in a nightgown and robe, was covered with Big Sarge's coat as they all headed out the door, back

Olivia Gaines

to the airfield. Technically, they could not take her from the city, but right now, Ryanne needed to be home.

Saxton was feeling the same way. It was time to head home for minute to reconnect with his own family.

Chapter 6. Reconnecting...

The flight to Dallas was quiet. Saxton watched his wife closely as she slept on the plane. Her head lolled from side to side with her jaw growing slack as drool seeped down the side of her face. *Yep. All that sexy belongs to me.* His eyes came up to find Ryanne watching them as he held his wife's hand. The glazed look he had seen earlier was gone and a sadness hovered in her eyes. Saxton muttered the words, "Be strong." She gave him a weak smile. Strength was really all she had at this point.

I'm not even wearing a bra. All of my clothes are in that house. Her life was in Corpus Christie. *I have to start over.*

It was no real surprise to any of them when Ryanne asked in a low voice, "Saxton, Odessa, can I stay with you guys for a few days?"

"Stay as long as you need to, Ryanne," Saxton told her. It was actually more perfect than either his wife or sister-in-law knew.

Odessa was a bit tuckered out from the early Saturday morning rising, the excitement, the worry and all of it was crashing down around her. It was 11:30 am and she was ready to head back to bed. So was Ryanne.

In the kitchen, he watched his wife try to feed her sister, who refused everything she saw in the fridge. Odessa piped up, "I will have you know that I have been taking cooking classes, and everything in there is tasty, well-seasoned, and delicious!"

"I will take your word for it, sis, but I'm not hungry," Ryanne told her as she cut her eyes sideways at Saxton.

Saxton tossed her an apple as he walked around the table and swooped his wife up into his arms. "Make yourself at home, Ryanne. I'm putting these two back in bed."

He carried Odessa up the stairs, sitting her gently on the bed. She was grinning at him as she began to remove her shoes. "You aren't slick, Saxton Blakemore. You're being all nice because you're trying to slip in some brunch since you didn't have any breakfast." She shimmied her shoulders as she took off her bra. Her breasts were growing fuller as each week passed as they prepared themselves to nourish their son in a few months. Saxton loved the changes in her body. The roundness of her belly, swollen with his son was a major turn on to him. *I did that. I planted that seed.*

"I know something else I would like to slip you," he said as he lay down beside her.

She laughed as she rolled to her side to face him. "I'm game if you are," she told him as her fingers trailed along his chest.

The crow's feet at the corners of his eyes crinkled. "I dunno, baby. The way I'm feeling right now, I may mess around and dent his little head."

"If I could see my panties, I would take them off and hurl them at you, but you are going to have to help me," she chuckled as she reached for her hips to grab the soft cotton.

"I have no problem helping you with anything, my sexy wife," he tugged at her underwear, pulling them down her thighs, over her knees, and down past her ankles. "My God, you are beautiful." His throat seemed to close as he found himself nearly gasping for air.

"Saxton, are you okay?" she asked as she reached for him.

He closed his eyes for a second to get a grip on the surge of emotions threatening to spill from his eyes. "If I'm to die today, Mrs. Blakemore, I want to leave this world remembering you in your finest glory, the beauty of your magnificent form in this light of the day." His fingers ran across the skin of her belly, their son inside, responding to the touch of his father's hand.

Odessa eyes misted. "I never get tired of hearing you say that to me, Saxton."

"I say it because you are the most beautiful woman I have ever ... oh hell," he said as he pulled her in his arms. "Enough talk," he said as he smacked her lightly on the ass, signaling that he was ready. He was tired of talking; all morning long there had been talking and he was hungry. Brunch was as good of an idea as breakfast.

After seeing Odessa's family rally around Ryanne, Saxton had the overwhelming desire to head home and hug his mama. He packed an overnight bag before informing his wife he would only be gone a few days. It was Thursday. He would be back on Sunday. Thanksgiving was next week, and he had a great deal to be thankful for and he needed to let his parents know.

In the kitchen, he stood next to Ryanne. "You can only take this one day at a time. You talk about it when you're ready, not a moment before. Okay?"

She nodded, her face still blank. Saxton told his sister-in-law, "I'm heading home for a few days, and I'm glad you're here. She could use the company."

It was also his hope that giving Ryanne something else to focus on would help her healing. There was plenty to get done. New orders had come in and needed to get boxed up and shipped to the customers. Odessa had taken off for almost two weeks to get everything caught up, but she spent more time napping than anything. He took a few extra minutes to make sure everything was settled before heading to the airstrip to catch a ride home with the pilot. Both the pilot and the stewardess had taken a brief layover to rest before refueling and heading back to Houston. Walking through the front door of the Busy B Ranch was going to really be a surprise to his parents.

Another surprise occurred when Odessa awoke. Ryanne had pan seared some chicken breasts and made a Southwest Cobb salad for them to eat. She had also gone into the office of Blakemore Imports & Collectibles and began expediting orders. All of which was completed in her tattered nightgown.

"How long have I been asleep?" Odessa asked.

"Almost three hours," Ryanne mumbled.

Odessa pulled her sister into a sideways hug, her belly preventing any head on contact. "After I totally inhale this salad, why don't you and I head out to buy you some clothes?"

"I have some stuff at the house," she said softly.

Since they both had homes of their own, they often referred to their parents place as *the house*. Odessa was certain that most of the items there were dated, smelled like mothballs, and were behind a wall that was covered with their parent's questions. Odessa had a mouthful of chicken when she asked, "Yes, that may be, but are you ready to answer questions from Mom and Dad?"

"Good point. Is there something here I can put on? I mean really," Ryanne said as she turned and lifted the back of her nightgown to show Odessa her naked ass. She opened the robe to show she didn't have on a bra. "I feel like I was on some episode of cops, dragged out of my house in my housecoat. All I'm missing are three curlers and a beer can!"

Odessa was grinning through teeth full of Romaine. "Yeah, you are missing the 'he won't hit me no damned mo!' line that accompanies the swig from the beer can." They both grinned for minute, sharing almost a private secret.

Ryanne bent quickly and wrapped her arms around her sister's neck. "Thank you." She kissed her cheek briefly and headed towards the guest bedroom. "I hope you have a pack of new panties, I am not wearing an old pair of yours!"

"If you are going to get all picky, you can go commando for all I care," Odessa yelled down the hall at her.

Olivia Gaines

Chapter 7. What is that … a tattoo or something?

It was the guitar strapped across his back that Ryanne noticed first. The second thing she noticed were all the women who were watching him, flirting and trying to get his attention. The last thing she noticed was that he was truly a good looking man with a lot of self-confidence. His sexuality was oozing from his pores and smacking her in the face to get her attention. He had it. The sexy guitarist was not looking at anyone but her. Odessa had disappeared to the baby section of the store as Ryanne pulled a few bras and packs of cotton undies from the shelf.

The sexy man walked over to her. "Are you sure you want to buy *those*. They don't seem like something you would wear for a spicy evening," he said to her.

Ryanne eyes were down, as if she were refusing to look at him. "A spicy evening? Thanks but I don't need any help."

He reached for her arm but pulled his hand away. The bruises on her face had his focus. "I only said something because you have a sadness in your eyes. Even if he is no longer in your life, you still have to plan for the future. *Those* are for planning a future as a nun."

She looked in her basket at the 8 pack of white cotton undies. They were horrific underwear. *Maybe I could buy something with a little color.* Ryanne looked up at him. "Why do you care?"

"You seem like a smart lady who is sad. I dig smart women, and I don't want to see you so unhappy," he said to her. He was surprised that there was a great deal of truth in his words.

A young woman in short shorts and a halter top walked up to him. She asked, "Are you like famous or something?"

He was polite as he dismissed the girl. He swung the guitar from his back and flipped it over and began to strum a few notes, singing a tune about a sad woman who did not smile. Ryanne was momentarily transfixed. The stranger finished the song and smiled at her as if they, too, were sharing a secret.

"You do know the best way to get over a man is to get under a new one," he said with dark eyes that almost smoldered.

"And you are mighty forward. A few strums of a couple of chords will not get me out of my panties nor under you," she said. She pointed to the pack of tidy whities. "Not even wearing *those*."

He gave her a smile so soft and lascivious that Ryanne took a step backwards. His words were caressing her like a lover in a darkened room. "I'm progressive. I'm okay with being under *you*. I am willing relinquish control over to you...."

Is this how it feels to be Odessa? She sure as hell was channeling her sister as she took his card. The sexy man told her he was on a modified tour of Texas, in Dallas tonight, then on to Austin, San Antonio, and then Houston.

"May I see your phone?" he asked her.

She handed it to him as he swiped the screen, found the camera, and stood behind her. The guitar was poking her in the butt. *Thank God it's just his guitar*. His arm came around her neck as he posed and took a selfie with her.

"So you can think of me tonight," he said, grinning as he started to walk away.

"I don't even know your name," she said as she looked

at the card that only held an image of his guitar and a phone number.

"I am Eduardo, but, when you ring me tonight, I prefer you to call me Eddie."

Ryanne was uncomfortable as the top button of his shirt slipped open. He had some sort of tattoo. She pointed to it. "What is that, a tattoo of something?"

Eddie stood still as he moved the guitar around to his back, the strap hanging about his neck. He opened three buttons of his shirt as several women stood close by watching. Using both hands, his fingers caressing the material, he pulled back the plain front of the shirt to show his chest.

Ryanne was squinting at the detail of the image etched into his skin. "What is that- a cobra?"

He was smiling at her. "No, my lovely smart lady, it is the head of a serpent."

Chapter 8. Mom, I'm home ...

Saxton walked into the front door of his childhood home feeling a sense of exhilaration. He still had keys to the front door, but as excited as he was to see his parents, he was more excited to ride his horse, Longshot. Lately, thoughts of moving back to Houston had been in the back of his mind, but Odessa's parents were also getting up in age. At least his brother and sister were here and interacted with Lucy & Bobby Ray on a daily basis. He only wished he could do the same.

"Mom, I'm home. Are you here?" he called into the cavernous living room. When he received no answer, he pressed one of the intercom buttons, which connected to every room in the house, including the lanai. "Mom, I'm home."

It was two in the afternoon and he knew his father would be heading home from the office soon. Since handing the reins of Blakemore Oil over to Connard, Bobby Ray, his father, seldom worked a whole day. Twice this year, they had been to Dallas to visit him and Odessa. The second time they came back, his mother, Lucy, had brought along the cook, Ralph. Odessa's cooking was improving, but his parents were not going to take any chances on being hungry from pushing food around on the plates of Odessa's very healthy meals. To her credit, the food was seasoned so much better, but there was still some panache missing. He had lost a few pounds, so he didn't complain.

"Saxie, is that you?" Grandma Patsy asked as she made her way down the hall. Saxton dropped his overnight bag and he moved quickly to embrace his grandmother. He enveloped her in his arms and lifted her from the floor.

"Oh, Saxie, be careful. You know I just turned 80. You will mess around and snap one of my damned hips!" she told him.

"I would never hurt you, Grammy," he said as he sat her down. He kissed her leathery cheek. "Besides, you're tougher than I am and I ain't even close to breaking a tough bird like you."

Lucille Blakemore came into the kitchen, a highball in one hand and a feather duster in the other. Saxton didn't know which one to look at first, his mother drinking in the middle of the afternoon or his mother with a cleaning apparatus in her hand. Lucy, as everyone called her, did not partake in any activity that remotely suggested anything domestic.

"Are you cleaning something, Mama?" he asked.

"In this lifetime, darling, no I am not," she told her eldest son as she pulled him into her arms. "What are you doing home? Is everything all right?"

She looked around him and so did Grandma Patsy. They were looking for Odessa. He grinned at them both. "She's at home. Everything is just fine. Can't a guy come home to see his two favorite girls?" He disengaged from his mother's arms and headed straight for the fridge.

Lucy sipped at her drink. "Saxton, you ain't fooling nobody. You came all the way to Houston to get a decent damned meal!"

She was looking at her mother over the rim of the highball glass, whispering to Patsy, "Lord knows that girl is as sweet and loving as the day is long, Mama, but she can't cook worth a flip."

Patsy's grey head wobbled to and fro. "Is that why you took the cook the last time you went?"

"Yes, and thank the Lord. I was not going to spend one more day eating a sautéed bean sprout, crunchy baked leaves of grass or a tofu anything," Lucy exclaimed.

Saxton pulled his head from the fridge with a rib covered in Bobby Ray's sauce shoved in his mouth. "Those were kale chips and I have never been healthier, Mama."

"Well goody-goody gum drops for you and your grass shitting colon, but I would swim to Hell and back for a piece of fried chicken, some duck fat potatoes, and anything slathered in whipped cream," Lucy said as she teetered into the dining room. Saxton and Patsy followed behind her, trying to see what she was doing with the feather duster.

The dining room was buzzing as the staff was pulling out silver to polish, counting place settings, and prepping for Thanksgiving next week. Lucy turned suddenly, looking at Saxton. "I just had the most brilliant idea!"

Patsy was mumbling under her breath, "I don't know how, with as much as you drink ..."

"I heard that, Mama," she said as she turned her back to her mother, ignoring the jibe. "Wouldn't it be wonderful if you and Odessa came home for Thanksgiving? We could give her a baby shower here next week." Her eyes and mouth were wide like she had just found a real life use for algebra.

The look on Saxton's face spit on her enthusiasm like a drunk man peeing on your leg in the subway. Lucy's mouth was downturned as she waved one of the young housekeepers over and handed her the glass to refill. "And why can't you come to Thanksgiving *this year*, Saxton?"

He was feeling bad about it because she was right – he

had not been home for the holidays in almost five years. "We were planning to have some friends over for dinner this year, Mama ... and then there are her parents...."

"And what about *your* damn parents? She is carrying my grandchild, too, you know," Lucy said with some resentment in her words. As her fresh drink arrived so did a fresher idea. "Why don't we send one of our planes up and pick up her, the parents, and whoever else you were planning to invite to your house. We will just invite them here. Lord knows we have enough room."

Patsy started to sputter. "You are inviting *all* of them *here?*"

Lucy was having no part of her mother's antics today. It was a 10,000 square foot house that was empty most of the time. Besides she was just on her second drink and it wasn't even five o'clock yet. "Good Lord, Mama, stop being ridiculous. The girl's family is just black, it's not like they are a bunch of Episcopalians."

"Ralph," Lucy yelled into the intercom. The cook came out of the pantry. "We are going to have a Thanksgiving feast. I need the largest bird you can get your hands on, I want a suckling pig, and I want some lamb roasted on a spit ..." she stopped and looked at Saxton. "How many people are we talking here, sweetheart?"

Saxton didn't know. He started to think it out loud.

Big Sarge.

Dora.

Kevin, Jr.

Agent Roget.

Ryanne.

He wasn't sure if Kevin, Jr. was going to bring Mary

Jean.

Odessa had invited Victorío and Antoinette.

Of course me and Odessa, which makes ...

"I would say add ten, Mama," he said.

She threw back her drink, sat the glass on the table and clapped her hands three times. "Okay, everyone, we have a slight change. We are now serving twenty for Thanksgiving dinner, which means we also have twenty heads to feed brunch and breakfast the next morning."

Saxton watched in amazement as she started calling out orders to the small staff to open the extra guest rooms and get fresh linens on the beds. She looked at Patsy. "Mama, let's make a list of all the people we want to have over for the shower. This is my first grandchild and I want the good shit for that baby, so leave those old cheap, dusty women from the missionary society out of this one."

Lucy stopped mid-stride and turned to look at her son. "Saxton, why are you home? You never did say."

He gave her a barbecue-sauce-covered kiss. "Because I missed you."

"That's sweet, honey. Mama missed you, too," she said as she went back to issuing orders.

It was amazing. When Lucy Blakemore had something to accomplish, a drink never touched her lips. It was another reason why he had considered moving back, so she would have someone to fuss over besides her mother, who spent more time fussing over her. Either way, it was going to be an interesting couple of days as all of those different types of people all sauntered through the front doors of the Busy B Ranch for dinner with the Blakemores.

Chapter 9. How did you get my number...?

The office for Blakemore Imports & Collectibles was clean. All of the inventory was sorted, shelved, and categorized. It took another two hours, but orders were matched with products that were sitting, ready to be boxed, labeled, and shipped. Her sister needed an assistant, especially with the baby arriving in less than three months.

A wave of sadness struck Ryanne as she took a seat in the chair behind the desk. The add-on room to the house wasn't fancy. It was kind of a storage unit converted to an office. Nothing about her sister's home was elaborate; she lived a normal, uncluttered life, in rooms filled with splashes of color. Based on the calculations in her head, along with the packing slips she had seen, her sister was easily pulling an extra thirty grand a year from this side business. More melancholy kicked her in the gut as she realized that she would not have a job after next week. There was no way she was going back to Corpus Christie and she sure as hell wasn't going to work in the same building as that man.

Several other issues started knocking her about as she sat staring at the wall. *Who hired Dwight to seduce and marry me so he could keep an eye on Saxton and Odessa?* The tears, which were clogging her tear ducts for the past two days, were pinching on her nerves. *I will not cry over him. I refuse. I may cry over losing my bogus artificial life, but I will get another one.* On Monday, she had decided, she would call her boss to resign. In the meantime, she had to start over. Her phone vibrated on the desk. She didn't recognize the number.

"Hello," she said into the line.

"Hey there, my lovely smart lady. I figured since I didn't hear from you last night, that I would touch base with you this morning," Eddie said into the line.

This was odd. She didn't remember giving him her number or her name for that matter. "How did you get my number?"

Eddie laughed into the phone. "I sent myself a text of the photo we took together. Besides, I had your number from the second I spotted you in the store."

Ryanne leaned back in the chair and crossed her legs. "And what do you believe you have dialed up, Eddie Casanova?"

His smile could almost be felt through the phone. "Eddie Casanova? I like that. I may change it to my new stage name."

They both were quiet. He spoke first. "I'm on the move a great deal in my line of work. Of course there are women who flock to me, and when I started, I will admit I partook of the offerings. After a few years of that, it gets boring."

"And what does that supposed to mean to me, Eddie?"

"Oh come on. You're smarter than that. What do you think I want from you?" he asked with some firmness in his voice.

"I honestly don't know. You are implying that you don't want random sex, yet meeting me was random," she told him.

"Nothing in this life is ever random, my sweet lady. We enter this life naked and scared and we hope to find another soul to share this existence, so that when we leave this plane, we are not naked and alone," he told her.

Ryanne found herself smiling. "So in other words, you

want to get naked and not be as scared as a small babe because every night you find yourself alone... And what am I to do about this loneliness that you pack up to travel with along this plane?"

"It is my hope that you stave it off," he said softly. "I'm not asking for much. Dinner, some intelligent conversation, a few embraces to wish me luck before I take to the stage. A few kisses when I come off of my set ... rub my ego, tell me I was great...."

She was laughing. "You sure aren't asking for much are you?"

"I am now asking for your name," Eddie said in the line.

"Ryanne," she paused. "Ryanne Trodat," she completed the sentence. She was also going to file for an annulment or something next week as well. The name Dobbins she no longer wanted associated with her name.

Eddie liked how well this was going. "Well, Ryanne, I am headed to Austin for a gig tonight, then on to San Antonio, a quick pop in Corpus Christie to handle an issue that has been causing me some grief, then I am in Houston for three days."

She said nothing.

"Ryanne," he called her.

"Yes, Eddie," she responded softly.

"Meet me in Houston on Tuesday?" he asked her.

"I'll think about it," she told him.

Eddie held the phone as he looked out the window of the small waiting area at the airstrip. "There is something else I want you to think about as well." He sat the phone down and picked up his guitar. He strummed a few chords and sang a soft melody. "I am really good with my hands and fingers, Ryanne."

"Oh my," she said in the line.

"I will see you on Tuesday," Eddie said as he hung up the phone.

Eduardo was pleasantly surprised when he spotted Odessa's sister in the store. He had not expected her to be an attractive woman with intelligence radiating through her eyes. Ryanne had a lovely figure, a warm smile, and a quick wit. She was not anything like Dwight had painted her to be. His intention had been to kill her, but he found himself liking the woman, and something about her sadness bothered him. *I am the cause of it, sending the wrong man to be her lover.*

Dwight had called her a cold fish in bed. There was nothing cold about her. In fact, she was quite the opposite. Maybe what he had said to her had far more truth in it that he wanted to admit. The mother of his children was a cold woman, not only to him, but to his four boys. The first five years of their marriage had been a test of his patience, and he wanted nothing more to do with her after she intentionally caused the birth defects in their youngest son. A woman like that he had no use for.

He didn't mind being a widower. He also had no qualms about being a widow maker. "Señor," his pilot called to him, "we are fueled and ready to head to Corpus Christie. You may board when you are ready."

He was more than ready. Dwight had lied to him about Ryanne. Eduardo was also wondering what else his informant had lied about.

Mariana was seated on the plane when he boarded. "Is everything okay, Señor?"

"No. My toe still hurts like hell and now I have to go

and personally kill someone else," he said as he plopped down in the seat and removed his boot. "I swear, with the exception of you, you just can't get good help these days!"

Odessa walked into the office as Ryanne ended the call. "Was that your attorney, Ryanne?"

"No," was all she said.

As Odessa's eyes scanned the room, a giant smile came over her face. "Wow! Thank you so much. I tell you, Ryanne, these last two months it seems like all I do is eat, sleep, and poop. I am so behind, and I could really use some help."

"Whatever you need, Odessa. I am glad to lend you a hand," she said.

"That is great news, because I just got off the phone with Saxton and he wants us all to come to Houston next week for Thanksgiving. I'm going to need your help convincing Mom and Dad," Odessa said.

"Houston? Next week?" Ryanne repeated.

"Of course, you are coming, as well as Kevin. I think Saxton said he invited Roget, Antoinette, and Victorío," she said. Odessa wrapped an *Artesanía* pot in with bubble wrap before she put it in a box with shipping popcorn. "I think it may be a nice change of pace for the holiday, and his folks really like to cook. Lots of good food," Odessa said.

She stopped talking when Ryanne walked up behind her and enveloped her in her arms. "Thanks, 'Dessa. Thank you for everything."

With a quick pat on her sister's arm, Odessa said,

"Anytime you are ready to talk, Ryanne, I'm ready to listen."

Ryanne only smiled as she thought of Eddie's words: *Nothing in this life is ever random.* Next week she would be in Houston. She saved his number in her phone and used the selfie for his profile picture.

Chapter 10. Ms. Blakemore, your appointment has arrived ...

Saxton had never cleaned out his closets in his old room at the ranch. Since losing a few pounds, most of the clothes still fit. He pulled out his charcoal grey suit, a white shirt, and a red tie. His father had been very surprised when he came home from work the day before and found Saxton sitting in the kitchen, munching on gingersnaps Patsy had baked earlier for him. They said little as he joined his father for a late evening ride. Even Longshot, his horse was glad to see him. At his request to his parents, he asked that they not tell his sister and brother he was home.

Today, he planned to surprise Belva by showing up at the office and taking her to lunch. He had called ahead and managed to get on her calendar because she was a very busy woman. Belva Blakemore was the philanthropic arm of Blakemore Oil. Last year, she took on the job full time after leaving the University. Her role in the company took care of the foundation, which supplied funds to Texas-based and national charities. Her offices were located on the sixth floor of the ten-story building.

Saxton hated the offices of Blakemore Oil. All the glass and shiny people who plastered on fake smiles as they kissed your ass because of the last name of Blakemore. He always resented being the oldest by default. Robert, Jr., was the eldest son, who died suddenly at the age of ten, and their mother was never the same. It was then that she began her afternoon sip fest of mint juleps. The less responsibilities she had, the more she drank. Her oldest son and heir was gone, Saxton became the heir apparent. Technically, the job of CEO of Blakemore Oil belonged to Robert, Jr. Saxton's role would have been to oversee the ranch, a job that was currently held by his Uncle Dusty, but he opted instead to leave home and make his own name. The name Blakemore carried a great deal of weight in Houston, and it was something he learned at a young age was not always a good thing. People disappeared at the snap of a Blakemore finger and the police looked the other way.

Belva's husband had disappeared. Saxton knew better than to ask questions. He never asked them of his sister, and she never asked any of him. As he entered the glass building, heads turned and snapped.

"Is that Saxton Blakemore?" one redhead asked.

"Saxton Blakemore just walked into the building in a suit," said some man with a large cup of coffee.

An older gentleman in a brown suit asked, "Is he finally going to take over the company?"

He could hear them all and he responded to no one. He rode up in the elevator in silence to the sixth floor. More heads turned as he made his way down the halls in his very expensive shiny black shoes and very expensive charcoal grey suit. What he was wearing now probably cost more than the right side of everything in his closet at home in Dallas. *I remember when this type of stuff was important to me.* What was important to him now was family.

"I have an 11:30 appointment with Ms. Blakemore," he told the assistant behind the very large wood desk.

She leaned forward with breasts too large for the small top she wore and pressed the button. "Ms. Blakemore, your 11:30 appointment has arrived."

Her Texas drawl could be heard through her office door as the scent of her overly expensive perfume arrived in the waiting area before she did. "I don't have an 11:30 appointment, Clara," she said as she flung open the door.

"Saxton?" she said with surprise as she looked at her big brother.

"Yes. I am your 11:30. Your calendar has been cleared until 2 pm and you, my dear sister, are all mine," he said to her. He extended his elbow. "Grab your purse and let's ride."

Her lips were moving but no sound was coming out. Saxton loved it. He dropped his elbow and moved around her to the drawer where she kept her purse. He grabbed it, pushed it into her hand, and pulled her towards the door. "We will be back at 2, Clara," he told the woman who was grinning at him like a basket case.

Belva still had not found any words even when they reached the lobby. Her inability to speak only worsened when Saxton walked over to open the door to his Grandmother's 1976 Cadillac Seville. It was probably the last time Patsy drove it as well. The car was a funky baby blue in color but in mint condition and ran like a dream.

"Saxton, what is the meaning of all this? You are wearing a suit. You walked in the doors of Blakemore Oil... taking me to lunch ... oh God! Is Mama about to die from cirrhosis of the liver?" Her cheeks were flushed and pink.

He pulled the car from the curb and drove to what he knew was her favorite restaurant. "No, sis. I'm in town to spend some time with my family. You have a new job title coming up and I just wanted to sit down with you one-on-one and spend some time," he told her.

"What new job title? This is all freaking me out!" she said to him as she ran her hands through her long mane of black hair.

"Belva, you are going to be an aunt in three months," he said as he glanced at her.

She was grinning. "Oh my God! That's right, Saxton, you are going to be a dad!" The conversation picked up between them as they shared childhood memories about Uncle Dusty, their aunts, and good times. Belva never complained about either of her brothers. They were good men and good to her. Even when she went through a phase of bad boys and not loving herself, her brothers were always there, pruning off the weeds which kept trying to take root around her.

Grandma Patsy had become a surrogate mother to them as their mother began to mix the pills with the highballs, and when Lucy's mornings started at noon. Belva, desperate for attention, sought affection from many of the wrong men. One, she even married.

Colton Hornsby was the worst kind of snake. A man of little to no character who made it obvious he only wanted Belva for her money. After whisking her away to Vegas, he was disappointed to find that Bobby Ray had tied the money up and only gave her enough to live on each month. Once the rent, her car note, and utilities were paid, there was little left over for anything else. Colton had to get a job to help support his wife. Yet the disappointment continued when he also found out that Bobby Ray was not going to give him a cushy job at Blakemore Oil, but instead gave him a field hand job on the ranch working with Dusty.

His frustration in not having access to the Blakemore bank was taken out on Belva. It started subtly at first, moving her further out and away from her family. Next, he started beating on her self-esteem, taking chunks of an already low self-confidence away. Saxton stayed in constant contact with his sister, as she shied away from their father. When Colton started laying his hands on Belva is when Saxton took exception.

It was also at 3:30 in the morning when she called him from the closet in the bedroom of the nasty little rat hole they called their home. Saxton arrived at the ratty apartment to find his sister beaten and bleeding. He believed it only fair to do the same for Colton.

The damage from that night lasted far longer than anyone had anticipated. The child that Belva was carrying did not survive. Neither did her ability to conceive another child in her lifetime. When Saxton carried her limp body to his truck, he left Colton's in the floor of the apartment. A call to his father from the hospital and that was the last anyone saw of Colton Hornsby. To this day, Saxton had no idea whether or not the man was dead or alive. A 3:30 am phone call changed his life.

The phone call from Ryanne brought back the ugly memory. The next few phone calls that arrived were going to bring back a few more memories for the Blakemores, as well as the Trodats. If there was one thing that Bobby Ray had taught him, if you see something once, it is random; you see it twice it is more than a coincidence. If you see it three times, it is a pattern and intentional. But Saxton had also learned on his own that there is no such thing as random.

Chapter 11. Who sent that box...?

Bucerias Nayarit, Mexico

Victorío sat in his office wishing for an escape. His current day-to-day operations were pummeling the joy out of his life and he needed a reason to smile. The American holiday of Thanksgiving was approaching and he had been invited to come to Dallas to have dinner with Saxton and Odessa. He wasn't so sure how he felt about the rest of the family. Odessa's mother was scary. The whole thing she did with the towels to his cousin, Mateo, was still haunting him when he closed his eyes at night. Dora Trodat was a terrifying lady.

It explained why the little slip of a woman Saxton had married was full of fire. He really respected Odessa. He esteemed Saxton even more. An individual may not be able to choose their family, but one did have a say in whom they befriended.

His family ... that was another story altogether. It panged him that since going legitimate with his business, he had earned more enemies than when he was a cutthroat drug dealer. He no longer had any desire to walk on the darker side of life, but he thrived on walking in the clear light of day. The thing that truly amazed him was to walk into a meeting and not have to worry about whether he would walk out alive. He'd seen it one time too many; a bad guy approaching an even worse guy who was tougher than the guy who walked in before. Either way, at the end of conversation, if there was one to be had, somebody was going to end up dead. Victorío wanted to make sure it wasn't him.

In the interim, he made alliances. He was not pleased

with how his relationship with the Nueva Generación had turned out, but Hugo Delgado had pretty much ended the partnership with that group. Trying to kill him was by any account a deal breaker. He still worked some with the Zetas, but that group was headed up by Delgado's brother, Eduardo. He was seldom seen and even Victorío was unaware how he looked after so many years. It was clear that he had sent Mateo to kill the Blakemores, but his cousin was more into pissing people off than actually doing as he was instructed. What worried Victorío the most was Mateo had probably pissed off the wrong person.

A yellow DHL truck made its way up the drive to the hacienda. *Antoinette. She has probably ordered something else she does not need.* To his surprise the box was for him. The weight of the container surprised him as he maneuvered the package to his office. *Who is sending me something?* Caution made him pause as he looked at the unmarked box. He put his ear closer, listening to hear if any ticking was made.

Hesitant, he slipped the letter opener into the sides and cut away the tape. Carefully, he opened the flaps to come in contact with lots of dry ice. He used the letter opener to push some of it to the side. The contents had a peculiar smell. There were packs of lime inside the box, along with coffee beans. Gently, Victorío moved these items aside.

Ay Dios Mío! He almost screamed as he peered into the box to see the severed head of his cousin, Mateo, staring up at him, with that same foolish grin he often wore. In his death, someone had made him go out wearing the duplicitous smile he presented in life to so many others.

There were no doubts in his mind that it was Eduardo

Delgado who sent that box. He would pack the car and go and visit his uncle before leaving for the United States. He would take him this horrible gift so he could bury his favorite son, or at least what was left of Mateo Rentería.

Corpus Christie, Texas

Dwight awoke with an uneasy feeling. It had been two days since Ryanne had shot him. As many questions as he asked, he was receiving even fewer answers. No one knew where she was; some had checked flights, trains, buses, and nothing. In two days, his wife had vanished. *I will have them expand my search to Dallas. Maybe she is with her sister.*

A more primary concern for him was his own well-being. *I have failed the head of the Zeta Cartel.* Even when he did get out the hospital, to kill Ryanne now would be premeditated murder. The extra he had been receiving each month to woo her was not enough to change his identity or to get out of the country. The idea of marrying her was his idea. Working with a shady insurance agent to take out an extra policy on her was also his idea. For any of his misery to pay off, he had to finish the job.

His eyes opened into the darkened room and he spotted a man sitting in the corner with a guitar. Throat dry and cracking, Dwight asked, "Who are you and what are you doing in my room?"

The man smiled. "I told them I was with The Healing Waters Therapy Mission. We provide music therapy to despondent patients."

I am not sad. Dwight tried to sit up but it was difficult. His loving wife had shot him in the nads. That alone, was enough to make him take her life, which he planned to do once he was recovered.

"I'm sorry, I am not depressed. I don't need you to sing or play for me," Dwight told the man.

"Are you sure you are not sad? You really should be. Especially knowing that you were given a job that you failed to complete," the man said. Dwight flinched in the bed. The guitar carrying man continued to talk as he strummed a few chords on the instrument.

"The problem with greed is you make a choice for what you think is easy money, but you never know who you are actually dealing with on the other end of the phone," the man told him.

Dwight began to mumble, stumbling over his words as the sweat began to bead on his forehead. He reached for the call switch for the nurse.

"I disabled that. You cannot call out for help," he said as he remained still in the chair, strumming his guitar.

"Who are you?" Dwight wanted to know.

The man began to sing a few words of a song he had never heard. "The real issue here, Dwight Darrel Dobbins, is that you lied to me. You told me your wife was an unattractive woman and a cold fish. You also were paid to woo her; not to marry the woman." The guitar-playing stranger stood, his face no longer in the shadows of the room.

"Señor Delgado," Dwight mumbled.

"*Sí*," he said with a smile. This man was far younger than Dwight had imagined him. The calm he exuded made him scarier than a cutthroat in a dark alley. From his back pocket, Eduardo removed a syringe, pulled back the plunger and injected an air bubble into Dwight's IV. "If you lied to me about how she looked, you probably lied about how she was in bed as well. That, I intend to find out for myself."

Eduardo watched the panic fill Dwight's eyes. Never one to be sadistic about death, especially when it was at his hands, he preferred for the end to be quick. This one, he wanted to hurt. He pulled out his phone and showed Dwight the selfie of him and a smiling Ryanne. "Yes, next week, I will show her how a real man makes love to a woman. When I am done, she will forget you ever existed. Besides, she will be rich from the insurance policies you decided you both needed. *Sí, Sí*, I know about that as well Dwight Darrel Dobbins."

Dwight grabbed at the IV, trying to pull it from his arm, but it was too late, the air bubble entered into his vein. Eduardo strummed his guitar as he left the room and walked down the hall of the ward. He stopped to play for a few of the nurses at the station when the code sounded in Dwight's room. Nurses were running and yelling for a code blue. Crash carts were flying on light wheels to Dwight's room as Eduardo calmly walked to the elevator and stepped inside the car.

Ryanne would be notified later today of her husband's death. He found it disconcerting that he wanted to be there to console her. His next stop was Houston and a quiet evening comforting an attractive young widow.

Dinner with the Blakemores

Chapter 12. Welcome to the Busy B ...

Kevin, Jr., or Kev as Odessa liked to call him, arrived home earlier than anticipated, which was perfect for the Trodats. A quick call to Saxton and the family met the plane at the same airstrip to fly to Houston on Tuesday evening. Aboard the aircraft, Kevin, Jr., who had been informed of the situation with his sister and Dwight, said nothing as he sat quietly, holding Ryanne's hand.

It also had not escaped Dora's notice that it was not the same plane they had taken a few days before. "Unless they changed the carpet and leather seat covers in three days, this is not the same plane. This one is swankier," she commented.

Kev piped up, "They have more than one plane? 'Dessa, how rich is Saxton?"

Odessa had little to say on the subject other than one comment. "Saxton and I have what we are building together."

Big Sarge grinned at her. "That is a good answer, 'Dessa, but his family is loaded. They have oil wells, oil rigs, Texas beef, horses, sheep, and everything else you can imagine. I cannot wait to see this ranch."

Dora spoke softly. "I can't wait to meet his mama. Do you think what I am wearing is okay?"

All three of her children shook their heads no. For the damndest reason, Dora was dressed like Barbara Stanwyck from the *Big Valley* television series. She wore a pair of suede culottes with a turquoise studded western belt, a turquoise silk blouse, a matching suede leather jacket with deep brown calfskin gloves. The gloves, of course, matched the knee high riding boots. Dora Trodat had never been near a horse in her life. To make it worse, around her neck she wore a scarf that was adorned in little beetles.

Kevin, Jr., asked, "Let me guess, you got that scarf from Mary Jean?"

Big Sarge asked what everyone wanted to know. "You still dating that weirdo?"

"Dad, that is not nice. Mary Jean is a middle school science teacher ..." Kevin tried to say.

Big Sarge interrupted, "So what? My sister is a high school English teacher; you don't see her walking around with pages from books hanging off of her!"

"Yes, but Daddy, she is always randomly quoting Shakespeare for no reason," Kevin added.

"What are you trying to say about your dear sweet auntie Kev?" Big Sarge wanted to know.

"I'm saying, Daddy. Your sister is a weirdo, too."

The room was quiet. "You have a point there, son," Big Sarge said as he slapped him on the back.

Kevin was still in defense of Mary Jean. "She is a sweet girl, but no ... the distance thing ..." Kev told his father and left it at that, saying no more.

It was also noticed that Ryanne had said no more about her circumstance with Dwight. "I don't want to talk about that right now," is what she told her family. They respected her wishes.

The flight was quick as they touched down on the east side of the ranch. A Suburban was there to meet them as the driver addressed Odessa, "Welcome home, Mrs. Blakemore."

Everyone turned to Odessa, who only rubbed her belly as she slid into the backseat of the vehicle and buckled her seat belt. It was less than a ten-mile ride from the east side of the farm to the front gates of the Busy B Ranch. The Trodats were all staring out the windows, watching the oil wells pump, some cattle graze as a few cowboys rode by the greener areas on horses. The vehicle entered the front gate of the ranch, driving down the one-mile stretch to the front door of the house. Ryanne's brow furrowed as she took in all that she was seeing.

"That is a big ass house! What is that 8,000 square feet?" Kev asked his sister.

Odessa felt uncomfortable when she answered, "I think it is 10,000 square feet."

"Whoa!" Big Sarge mumbled.

As the vehicle came to a stop, the crisp November wind whipped across the portico as an ominous sign of change being swept into their lives. The thunder of hooves could be heard, as in the distance, the cowboys they saw earlier were riding up to the house. It was easy to spot Saxton, sitting tall atop Longshot, the big black stallion's mane whipping in the wind as he rode up the path to greet them. The horse had barely stopped when Saxton slid out of the saddle to swoop Odessa up in his arms.

"Hey you," he said as his mouth found hers. "I missed the heck out of you," he said as he held her close, careful not to squish her belly. Longshot must have missed her, too, because the horse came over and nudged her purse.

"Fine. Fine. Give me a minute, you big brute," she said to the horse. Odessa fumbled through her purse to pull out an apple and fed it to the animal, who nodded its large head and walked away.

Saxton called after his horse, "Don't you wander off. I'll take you to the stables in a minute."

The horse didn't seem to give a shit about what Saxton was saying as it munched happily on the treat Odessa had given it. Saxton's attention went to his in-laws as he passed out hugs and shook hands while proclaiming loudly, "Welcome to the Busy B!"

The front doors opened as Lucy walked out, followed by Grandma Patsy. "Saxton, don't be rude, let the people come inside and warm themselves by the fire. And get that damned horse out of here before it shits all over my driveway!"

"Sorry, Mama," he told her as he introduced Odessa's family to his own. He told the Trodat's "Don't worry about trying to remember names. There will be so many Blakemores in and out of this house in the next few days, there is no way you guys will be able to keep up with everyone."

Saxton's phone was ringing as he fumbled in his pockets to grab the device. Big Sarge had his eye on Grandma Patsy, who was giving him the evil look. Lucy's arm was linked into Dora's as she ushered her through the front doors. The driver was taking care of their luggage as the rest of the riders rode up. Bobby Ray was among them as he slid down to embrace Odessa, shake hands and welcome everyone to the house. It was not hard to see the resemblance between Saxton and his father. The same height, the same build and same hair, only Bobby Ray's was a deep grey.

Odessa's eyes were on Saxton, who was obviously receiving some bad news on the phone. Her eyes were imploring him for answers but his eyes wandered to Ryanne. It was the look on her husband's face that told her Dwight was dead. She didn't even need to ask. The real task was going to be telling Ryanne. It was no doubt that she wasn't going to take it well.

Lucy was prattling on, "I sure hope you guys are hungry. Ralph, the cook, has been busy preparing something for you guys to graze on ..."

Grandma Patsy was watching Big Sarge. She sidled close to him. "I hope you like chili. I made a large pot of my famous Texas Busy B chili."

Big Sarge didn't trust the old woman, but she had just privately issued him a challenge. She was almost daring him to eat it. *I am a combat war veteran.* There was no way some old lady was going to issue him a challenge and he not accept.

"I will take a large bowl of your chili, Ms. Patsy," he told her as they entered the kitchen, which made Dora inhale her breath.

Ryanne watched the entire scene and was filled with mixed feelings. The home was lovely and Odessa had been welcomed as if she was the lady of the manor. Saxton grew up in all of this and so would Odessa's son, as well as any other children she would give him.

It isn't fair.

Odessa was going to inherit the kingdom and all she was left with was a man who married her for a monetary payment. It was insulting, humiliating, and a denigration of everything she worked hard to earn. It wasn't even clear how much she had been purchased for, which was even more insufferable. *I went to college. I studied hard. I started my career late, but I got married. I was working towards a vision.*

This nightmare of a life wasn't her dream.

Dwight wasn't her dream.

Ryanne's phone buzzed. It was Eddie. A simple text message came through that said he was in Houston.

She responded back to him. *So am I.*

As he told her earlier, nothing is random.

Chapter 13. Dear Lawd ...

While Saxton was rubbing down Longshot, Lucy showed everyone to their rooms. Odessa pulled her mother-in-law to the side. "Ms. Lucy, my father has a bad hip. Is there a room downstairs for my parents?"

Lucy waved her hand. "Oh, pooh, girl! You do know we have an elevator!" Lucy pulled Big Sarge into it as everyone else climbed the grand staircase. Odessa reached the landing and could feel the tug at her lower belly. *Maybe I need to take the damned elevator, too.* Each day, the changes in her body were dictating the limitations of her condition. She rubbed her tummy. "Mommy is tired, baby. You are taking a lot out of me."

Lucy stepped from the elevator at the end of the hall, dragging Big Sarge behind her. The three bedrooms on the right side of the hallway were open, fresh, and ready for their new guest. What was new was the nursery. Odessa's eyes were wide as Lucy opened the door next to Saxton's room. "We haven't had a nursery up here in years. I was so excited. I had Dusty get started on it. I am just waiting for you to pick out patterns and wallpaper this week, so we can have it done!"

The giddiness of Lucy was new. Her mother-in-law not having a drink in her hand was also something new. Her exuberance was contagious. Even Dora was pulled into it. "Odessa, this is exciting. Have you even finished the nursery in your own home?"

In truth, she had not given it much thought, nor had Saxton put any effort into it, because in her heart, she knew, her husband was going to have to come home at some point. It seemed as if he was waiting for the right time to tell her, just as she was waiting for the right time to tell Ryanne how her life was going to change.

"Well, don't just stand around, y'all! There is a kitchen full of good food to eat, stories to tell, and a baby shower to plan for tomorrow!" Lucy exclaimed.

Odessa was still standing in the door of the nursery. *I am going to be a mother*. She absentmindedly rubbed her tummy. *In that chair is where I will nurse and sing to you.* Tears welled in her eyes as her brother and sister both flanked her; Kevin's arm around her shoulder and Ryanne's arm around her waist. It was Kevin who spoke first. "I am going to be the world's best uncle."

"And I am going to be the world's best aunt," Ryanne added.

Her head still low, and fingers on her tummy, Odessa said through her sniffles, "I am going to be the world's best mom."

Saxton arrived at the top of the stairs, winded but anxious to speak to his wife. "Yes. You will be, Mrs. Blakemore," he said as he leaned against the wall. He grinned at them. "Guys, give me a few minutes to get showered and changed and I will give you a tour of the ranch," he told Kevin and Ryanne as he took Odessa by the hand.

In the privacy of the bedroom, behind closed doors, he kneeled in front of his wife and kissed her belly. "I know it was only a couple of days, but it felt like forever. I have gotten so spoiled lying down each night beside you, and waking up to you each morning...."

Odessa's fingers ran through his hair. "Saxton, are we

ready for this?"

"We are as ready as we will ever be," he told her.

"Your mom is working on the nursery...."

It was the way he exhaled that made her pause. "Odessa.... At some point, I have to come home. My family will live in this house. Our children will grow up on Blakemore land, eat Blakemore beef, and learn how to take care of the earth as we pull from it Blakemore oil. I was sitting in a saddle before I could even walk on my own...."

His eyes beseeched hers for understanding. "I didn't want the company. I succeeded that to my brother, but the ranch ... I am the heir to all of this...."

His hand rubbed her stomach.

Odessa understood it all. "And he is the heir apparent?"

Saxton rarely discussed his family, or the details of why he left home. She was never clear on what he was running from, but figured in time he would tell her. "Belva can't have children," he said softly. There was something in his eyes that she could not read.

"And Connard? He will produce Blakemore heirs as well, right?" she asked him.

Saxton shook his head no, then thought about it and shrugged.

Odessa didn't understand.

"I thought he and his wife were planning to have some children this year?" Odessa said to her husband who had turned away. He was pulling socks and undies from his chest of drawers, which meant he was shifting the energy in the room and closing the conversation.

"Saxton, what are you not telling me?"

He turned to her. "Well ... his wife is his beard."

She knew it took a lot for him to admit that to her, as if he was breaking his brother's confidence. Odessa moved the conversation on to another subject. "...And what are you not telling me about Dwight?"

It wasn't random. He knew it wasn't random. "Your sister's bullet didn't kill him."

Odessa stood up from the bed. "Then who did?"

"No one knows. His heart stopped. Some people in the hospital mentioned a dude playing a guitar, but the funny thing is, no one can remember what he looks like," Saxton told her.

They both knew what it meant. A new player had entered the game and was cleaning up loose ends. It was going to be important for Ryanne to start talking and tell them why she shot her husband.

What did she learn that she was also not telling them that could be the difference between life and a quick death?

In the middle of the night, cries could be heard from down the hall. Neither Odessa nor Saxton were heavy sleepers and both were up with weapons drawn, bullets seated in the chamber, as they tiptoed down the hall, following the muffled cries. Initially they both thought it was Ryanne finally letting go of the pain, but it came from the room her parents were sharing.

Saxton tapped lightly at the door. It was opened by a much-frazzled Dora, who looked like she had been put through the ringer. Odessa asked, "Mom, what's wrong?"

Dora pointed to Big Sarge who was prostrate on the bed, moaning. "Sir," Saxton said. "Are you in pain? Do I need to call for a doctor?"

Big Sarge flopped over to his back. He had been crying. In all her life, Odessa had never seen her father cry. He was rolling back and forth on the bed.

"Daddy, please tell us what is wrong?" She begged of her father. He wiped away his tears, as he struggled to sit up on the bed, but gave up and plopped back down. "I stepped on a live mine coming down the Ho Chi Minh Trail in Nam. I took shrapnel in my side and still carried my buddy five miles, uphill both ways, to safety. And today I am going to die from a distended asshole from eating that woman's chili!"

Big Sarge grabbed at Saxton's gun. He cried out, "Kill me. Make this pain stop." A loud gurgle could be heard from his belly as he scrambled to get to his feet. Saxton hoisted him off the bed and half carried the man to the bathroom door.

"Dear Lawd!" They heard Big Sarge yell as his stomach gurgled while his bowels released a puff of methane followed by a sound that Odessa had experienced herself when she ate Grandma Patsy's chili.

Dora stared at the wall, mumbling, "I told that old fool not to eat that damned chili. You know your father, he loves a challenge."

That was not the only challenge they were going to face in the next few days.

Chapter 14. Courage and grace...

Wednesday morning was full of hustle and bustle. The baby shower was going to be at 1 pm and Lucy was barking orders like a mad woman. The meat had arrived for Thanksgiving and the kitchen was in chaos. Saxton grabbed Kevin, Jr., by the back of the shirt, told him to grab a jacket, and to follow him. Bobby Joe was leading the way.

Dora and Big Sarge were sleeping in after the night of pain, which left Odessa to talk to Ryanne at the kitchen table.

"Ryanne, we have not talked about what happened that night," Odessa opened the conversation.

"And we don't need to ... not today, not tomorrow, not ever," she told her sister as she sipped at her tea.

Odessa had to break the news to her. "I understand that it must be painful for you...."

Ryanne's eyebrows shot up. "Oh do you really?"

"If I am pissed off enough to put a bullet in a man, or it has come to the point I have to put a bullet in a man, then yes, I do understand. Either it was your life at stake or he just didn't deserve to live. But, you didn't kill him, Ryanne, so there is something you are not saying," Odessa said to her with some serious concern.

It was true. The wound was still too raw and she was not about to tell her sister such horrific news. Not today. Today was all about the baby and Odessa's shower. She would not ruin it for her.

"Ryanne, it is important that you talk to me," Odessa said it more firmly this time.

"No. It is not. I don't want to hear another word about that man. I wish he would just die and be gone from my life forever!" she said through gritted teeth.

Odessa took her hand. "Ryanne ..."

As sisters, they were always able to communicate with each other without saying too much. Ryanne always had her head in a book whereas Odessa was always following her father about until Kevin was born and able to toddle around. There were very few secrets between the sisters. Never had they fought over a boyfriend or clothing as they were very different people who did not have the same interest in clothes or men.

"Something bigger is at play here and if you know something, it may be best to tell us what happened. What made you shoot him...?" Odessa asked.

"What do you mean something bigger may be at play?" Ryanne wanted to know.

Her lips were pursed as she exhaled, still gripping her sister's hands. "It's Dwight."

Ryanne snatched her hands away. "What about him?"

Odessa shook her head no.

No meant a great deal of things in the world of finance. A head shaking in that manner could mean the stock market has crashed and everything you had was gone. It could mean that the investment you made did not pay off. It could mean so many things.

"Are you telling me my husband is dead?" Ryanne asked.

Odessa reached for her hands again, hoping to give her sister strength, but Ryanne rose and took the plates to the sink. A lady in a housekeeper's outfit took the dishes from her shaking hands. Odessa rose to follow, but Lucy came into the kitchen, still barking commands.

"Odessa, I need you to drive Mama to the bank, then over to the mercantile, please. Now! Chop chop!" Lucy said as she pulled Odessa up from the chair. "Here, take my car." She placed the keys to the red Cadillac in their hands.

"Hurry up and get back here soon," Lucy commanded as Odessa followed Grandma Patsy out the back door.

Lucy looked at Ryanne. "And you. Stop moping about and come over here and lend me a hand getting the drawing room set up for the shower today. You will be in charge of helping your sister open gifts and the like."

Ryanne didn't argue, but set about doing the tasks she was assigned. Just like the good girl she was. Always doing as she should. Always doing as she was told. Go to college. Find a nice man. Get married.

I am a fucking widow. Yet in Odessa's world I am nothing more than an accessory, a convenience. There was a frustration building in Ryanne. So much had happened in such a short time that it seemed as if her brain was starting to fizzle out. Just get through this stupid shower and Thanksgiving.

That's all I need.
One day at a time, Ryanne.
Courage and grace, Ryanne.
Courage and grace.

It was 9 am and the men were in the stables, saddling up for a mid-morning ride. Today would be Kevin, Jr.'s first riding lesson. Dusty Blakemore brought out the chestnut colored mare for the young man to ride. The horse was looking at Kevin and he was looking at the horse. Neither seemed too fond of the other.

Uncle Dusty was nothing like his brother, Bobby Ray. He was more like the anorexic comedic version. He too stood at six-foot-two, had the same dark features, black hair with deep brown eyes, but he weighed almost 60 pounds less. Bobby Ray was more pragmatic in his approach to life, whereas Dusty could see humor in any situation. He watched Kevin closely as he moved to the horse, hesitantly reaching for the mane, touching the hair, allowing it to run through his fingers.

Dusty clucked his tongue and the horse turned, startling Kevin. "Damn it, son, you aren't asking it out on a date. I mean you're going to give her a ride and a good work out, but it's not as if she is going to call you later!"

Kevin was almost blushing. "I know. She is just so big. Do you have anything smaller I could ride?"

"Sure thing," Dusty told him. He walked away only to return with a Shetland pony. "Either you ride that mare or this little gal here, but whichever way, you are going to need a set of balls to put in the saddle. Do you need to go and get yours from your suitcase?"

"Sir..." Kevin started to say to him.

Dusty held up his hand. "Don't sir me ... most of the time I am elbow deep in horseshit, cow shit, or my brother's shit. Life is short. Get your ass up on that horse, give it everything you have and if you hate it, then so be it. But at least you tried, you did it, and you have a story to tell to the fellas back in the dorms."

Kevin could not argue with that logic as he mounted up and Dusty led the horse around the stables to where Saxton and Bobby Ray were waiting to start the morning ride. The men were quiet as they rode over the land toward the back stretch of the ranch. A few calves had wandered down too far and Saxton began to round them up and move them back towards the main herd. The smell was too much for Kevin who started to gag. Once he started to heave, the horse could sense something was wrong, became skittish, and reared up. Bobby Ray, quick as a flash was behind Kevin, catching him and throwing him across his lap on the saddle. The horse, who seem to have had his fill of the untrained rider, had run off back to the stables.

"Son, I hope you have better hands with women," Bobby Ray said as they turned back towards the main house, cutting the ride short. Kevin was still slung across his lap, face down on Bobby Ray's big sorrel-colored horse.

Bobby Ray looked over at Saxton. "...And you. You never said to your mama or me why you just popped up all of a sudden. What is going on?"

Saxton smiled when he answer his father, "I missed you."

"Ain't buying it. What is going on with you, son?" Bobby Ray asked again.

His dad was a no-nonsense kind of man. Beating around the bush only pissed him off, so Saxton came at him straightforward. "I was a shitty kid and an even worse teenager. Through all of it, you never faltered or changed how much you loved me or backing me up even when you know I did wrong. Now, I am about to be a father." He got quiet as the house came into view, the weight of the size of it no longer scaring him.

"Dad, I can only hope to be as good of a father to my children as you have been to us," he said.

It was a rare moment when Bobby Ray showed emotion, but today he was choked up. "I only wanted my children to be happy. I am never sure if you are ... Belva ... Connard ..." He choked up more when he said Connard's name.

"He can be happy, Dad, if you hadn't forced him to marry." Saxton said this out loud. It was one of the things he had wanted to say to his father for years.

"If he didn't, he would be excommunicated from the church and go to Hell for his life choices," Bobby Ray said.

Kevin, still face down on the horse, lifted his head. "Sir, if we all went to Hell for our life choices and poor decision making, there would be no one in Heaven."

"That may be true young man, but the Church is not as forgiving," Bobby Ray said to them both.

"Sir, the Church can't get you into Heaven, it is what is in your heart that will. Besides," Kevin said as he slid off the saddle. "You stop sending them checks every month, the Church will see things your way."

Bobby Ray stopped and looked down at him. Kevin was smiling.

"Does Connard go to church on a regular basis and is he active in the church's ministry?" Kevin asked.

Both Saxton and Bobby Ray were shaking their heads no.

"Well it seems like you are keeping up appearances for someone who doesn't really care what those people think, especially since he has nothing to do with them," Kevin dusted off his shirt. "I'll walk back to the house, Sir. If Dusty asks what happened, tell him I went to find my other set of balls. This pair is hurting."

Saxton sat watching Kevin walking away. Bobby Ray watched him waddling back to the house. He spoke to his son, "He seems like an interesting young man."

"You have no idea, Dad," Saxton said. His brother-in-law had really grown up in the past few months. He had seen Kevin exhibit courage when it was needed and grace as he helped others. The young man was a rare breed. Saxton was proud to be related to him, even if it was by marriage.

Chapter 15. Being Mrs. Blakemore ...

It was a quiet ride to the bank as Grandma Patsy clutched her purse while staring out of the window. Odessa was careful as she watched her speed and obeyed all the laws to arrive at the small bank in one piece. She quietly followed Patsy into the bank and took a seat in one of the waiting chairs. A young man who spotted them walking in began to trip over himself to get to Patsy. Odessa rose in defense and moved closer to her Grandmother-in-law.

"Ms. Sterling. I wasn't expecting you today. I see you have a new driver," he looked at Odessa, then at her belly, his brain obviously trying to comprehend why a pregnant black woman was driving the bank's best customer around.

"Harold, you insipid ass, that is my granddaughter-in-law. She is Saxton's wife, and she is carrying my great grandson," Patsy said with far more pride than Odessa expected. The look on her face said as much. The same look was on Harold's face.

"Stop dawdling, Harold, I need to get to my safety deposit box," she said as he led her away.

As Odessa went back to the waiting area, she was flanked by bank workers offering her sodas, water, fruit, and snacks. "Is there anything you need, Mrs. Blakemore?"

"What can we get for you, Mrs. Blakemore?"

"I will be honored to be your personal banker and assist you with managing your assets and credit cards, Mrs. Blakemore." A business card was shoved into her hands.

One young lady even brought out a pillow as she lifted Odessa's feet from the floor to slip it under her heels.

Odessa's hands went up. "Please stop. I am fine, thank you," she told the workers. She even handed the young lady back her pillow.

That wasn't the weirdest portion. A young Mexican girl came out and asked her, "May I please have your autograph?"

"No," Odessa told her in disbelief. The odds of her signature being used in all sorts of ways were too innumerable for her to count. There was no means to calculate the probability of it being used for something else. "I am not famous. You don't need my autograph," she said softly to the young lady.

Harold sidled over. "I am so sorry for mistaking you for someone else...."

"You mean mistaking me for the help?" she said flatly.

"I am so sorry, Mrs. Blakemore. Saxton and I went to school together, I don't want him to take any offense. Please don't tell him I inadvertently insulted you," Harold said.

"Honestly, I don't even know who you are other than Harold at the bank," she told the shaking little man.

"I am the branch manager. I mean, I am so sorry. I meant no harm. I don't want to disappear, too," he said with fear in his eyes.

"What are you talking about, Harold?" Grandma Patsy said as she returned from the vault. "Stop pestering her and go and lock my stuff back up!"

Harold was still mumbling his apologies as Grandma Patsy was walking out the door, her purse clutched tight to her chest. It was a weird interaction between her and Harold, but it got stranger at the mercantile store. It was as if everyone in the bank had called ahead, and no matter which street she turned down, people were waving at her, shouting, *Hey there, Mrs. Blakemore. How are you doing today, Mrs. Blakemore?*

Odessa hated it.

Everyone knew who she was yet she knew none of these people. It also didn't help to be driving a candy apple red Cadillac with the Busy B brand on the license plates. The weirdness worsened as she entered the mercantile and people were snapping photos of her like amateur photogs. She moved to the back of the store while she waited for Patsy. Odessa noticed a bluegrass basket on a top shelf. In her mind she was tall enough to reach it. In reality, she needed a step stool.

"You shouldn't reach over your head that way. I am told it increases the chances for the cord to wrap around the baby's neck," she heard a man say. He was a good-looking guy with a guitar on his back. "Here, allow me," he told her.

The basket was full of dust and probably had been on that shelf for years, but it was solidly crafted and would be great for holding baby towels in the nursery. "Thank you," Odessa told him.

"You are welcome, Mrs. Blakemore," he said to her with a smile. It could not come as a shock to her that he knew her name. Everyone in the store seemed to know her damned name. Hell, everyone in the little town knew her name.

"Please call me Odessa," she told him.

He extended his hand for a shake. "I am Eddie, musician extraordinaire." He flipped her hand over to kiss the back.

Odessa took the basket to the counter while she waited for Patsy. "I would like this basket, please. Can you clean it up a bit for me?"

"Oh you can have this one, Mrs. Blakemore," the clerk told her.

"No, the price says $35. I will pay the asking price," she told the girl, who seemed surprise.

Eddie was watching her. "You could have gotten the basket for free, yet you did not accept it."

"Nothing in the world is ever free, Eddie. Besides, I am not that kind of a person," she told him.

"What kind of a person are you, Mrs. Blakemore?" he asked.

It was a weird question coming from a stranger, but eyes were watching and ears were listening. "I am a hard worker, Eddie, and so is my husband. I treat others as I wish to be treated."

She could hear Patsy wrapping up in the background. The clerk came back with the basket as Odessa paid the price along with tax. The clerk seemed disappointed. "I wanted to give you that as a baby shower gift."

"Finding this basket in the back was a treat. You cleaning it up so nicely is gift enough," Odessa told her.

This woman is nothing like I imagined. Eddie found her intriguing, but to him, Ryanne was prettier. Odessa possessed a quiet power that radiated through her pores, but her sister was the type of woman you could lose yourself in. "Mrs. Blakemore, I am a traveling musician. I like to take selfies with people I meet along the way to show my kids. Would you be so kind and indulge me?"

"Of course," Odessa said as she took the picture with him.

Eddie watched her from the side of his eye. "Maybe you should take one of us with your phone as well. That way, when I am a famous musician, you will have a photo to show your little one," he told her. Odessa pulled out her phone and snapped a photo of the two of them.

"Odessa, it's time," Grandma Patsy told her as she walked over to hand the keys to the Caddy back to her. She looked Eduardo up and down, frowning in distaste. He stood beside the old woman and snapped a picture with her as well. The look Patsy gave him changed his facial expression.

It was the countenance on his face that made Odessa look at his hands. There were no visible snake tattoos. The feeling of danger came over her as she linked her arm into Patsy's. "Let's head home, Ms. Patsy. The family will wonder what has happened to us if we're gone any longer."

Odessa nodded her head to Eddie and said goodbye to the store clerk. She cranked up the Caddy and pointed it towards the Busy B.

"Odessa, you should not interact with the public in such a way. It is simply common," Grandma Patsy said.

It may have been, but Eddie was not. Patsy's dismissal of him sparked an anger in the man that was anything but the normal reaction of a traveling musician. His response was uncommon, which meant he was someone of importance. Patsy had treated him as a peasant and he didn't like it.

He wasn't randomly in that store to buy something.

He was in that store to meet Mrs. Blakemore.

He was there to meet me.

Eddie intentionally took pictures with me.

She started to calculate the usages of such a personal photograph. A random stranger in such close proximity to her.

It was taken as a threat.

The photo would be used as a threat to Saxton.

Shit.

She had walked into a trap and she was also going to be the bait.

There was one thing that niggled at her more than anything and kept flooding into her mind as she broke the speed limit getting back to the ranch. The easy ride into town was replaced with an 80 year-old woman holding the oh shit bar as Odessa rounded the curb on two wheels coming up the inside lane to the house.

How the hell did Eddie know she was going to be in that damned store?

Something else was troubling her as well.

There is no such thing as random.

Chapter 16. Are you frickin' kidding me...?

By the time she dropped Grandma Patsy off at the front door and went to park the car, most of the guests for the baby shower had arrived, along with Agent Roget and many of Saxton's cousins. Agent Roget tipped his hat before handing it to the butler. People she didn't know were hugging her while bestowing felicitations and touching her belly. Odessa needed to speak with her husband, but Dusty yelled, "All the fellers follow me!"

Saxton waved goodbye as he was pushed down the hall and Odessa was ushered into the front parlor, plopped into a chair, and handed something that tasted like fizzy lime sherbet. One sip was all it took before she handed it to her sister. A fleeting thought flashed across her mind of the stranger in the store having something to do with Dwight....

"I'm sorry, what did you say, Ms. Lucy?" Odessa found herself repeating. Lucy was passing out pens and paper. Belva was serving up more of the horrible punch. Her mother was greeting guests as they came through the door. Everyone seemed like they were ready to have a great time. Everyone but Ryanne.

Dwight is dead. She didn't know whether she was angry that he was dead and she didn't get her revenge, or that someone had killed the bastard before she had a chance. *I had my chance and let it go. I can't complain, but I am a widow.* That was the part that she could not wrap her mind around.

Well, that was until Odessa started to open presents.

Each present was grander than the last. Someone gave the child Microsoft stock shares. Another gave him stock shares in Coca-Cola. There were envelopes stuffed with money. There were large envelopes stuffed with checks. Some lady had hand-knitted a blanket out of Mohair. There were silver rattles. Gold pacifiers. Silk burping cloths. There was even shit she couldn't pronounce. Ryanne thought it had gone too far when some lady in a stuffy suit presented the child with a seat in the kindergarten class at some poo-poo chi chi school, when the child turned six! *Dear Jesus the child isn't even here yet and he is more relevant than I am.* The final blow for Ryanne came when Grandma Patsy presented her gift.

The child was given an oil well.

A what?

An oil well?

An oil well set to start production the day he inhaled his first breath of air.

"Are you frickin' kidding me?" Ryanne yelled aloud. Everyone in the room looked at her in disbelief. "AAARRRRRRGGGGGHHHH!" she screamed as she started kicking loose pieces of wrapping paper. Odessa stood up.

Her sister didn't do outbursts.

"I have got to get the hell out of here before I lose my goddamned mind!" Ryanne screamed.

"Somebody hand me some car keys and something with a GPS so I can get the fuck out of Southfork!"

Lucy handed her the keys to her Caddy. "Please do not bring my car back on E." Odessa's mother-in-law, forever the consummate hostess, gently pressed Odessa's shoulder to sit back down in the chair. She did not miss a beat as she drew everyone back into the party and away from Ryanne's meltdown. "Okay, so I think my mother's gift topped everyone's in the room," Lucy laughed as she made eye contact with Dora. "Let's continue with the gifts, then we'll have cake, and there are more games to play with gifts to win."

Dora was already half out the door, trying to catch Ryanne. "Baby, wait, please wait."

"Wait for what, Mama? I have been waiting for something all of my life. I finally get married to a nice guy ... or at least I thought he was, and he turned out to be the worst person on the planet." She looked at her mother as she grabbed her purse. Her coat she was struggling to put on so she opted to wear it like a cape. "And now he's dead. Murdered by someone who ..." she stopped talking.

Ryanne turned her back to her mother. "I need to breathe. I will get back before we ... I'll be back!" She stormed out the back door and found the garage. There had to be 20 cars inside the building, everything from antiques to modern marvels.

"How much money do these fucking people have?" Lucy's Caddy was up front. She climbed into the car, turned on the GPS. She plugged in the word bar and hit GO.

The voice on the system began to speak. "Drive one mile down Blakemore Lane. Make a right on Blakemore Boulevard."

"Are you fucking joking?" The tears were threatening to overrun her common sense when her phone chimed.

It was a simple message.

The Carriage Suites. Room 427. – Eddie.

She added the hotel address into the GPS and followed the instructions. She didn't know what she was doing. It didn't matter, either, because she was going to do it anyway. She would deal with the consequences later.

Little did she know how vast and longstanding her actions, for this night would be.

Chapter 17. You know why you are here ...

Why am I here?
What am I doing?
I shouldn't be here.

These words danced about Ryanne's head as she stepped off the elevator onto the fourth floor of the Carriage Suites. She sent a text message to Eddie.

I am here.

Her stride was slow as she walked down the corridor, her coat buttoned up to the collar. The footfalls on the thick carpet could barely be heard as she read the room numbers. The courage she had getting out of the car had all but left her when her phone pinged.

The door is open.

Just like that. She was about to cross over a threshold of no return. Out of habit and good parenting, she tapped lightly at the door of room 427, before pushing it open to let herself inside. Uncertain of what to expect, he was standing by the window, drinking a glass of ice water. Eddie wore no shoes, a pair of black jeans, and a red shirt held together with one button at the center. His jet black hair was damp and slicked back on his head.

The smile he gave her made her feel at ease. "Good evening," he said to her. "Please lock the door."

Ryanne turned the bolt to secure the door. A deep inhalation was taken as she turned back around to find him still standing at the window. His movements to her were slow. "Let me take your coat," he said.

She unbuttoned her favorite coat to hand it to him, and he stood for a moment to snap a mental photo of her. The pretty blue dress she wore was flattering to her figure. It was classy, like the lady. Eddie's hands went to her hair and pulled out the pins she used to wear it up off her shoulders. It fell loosely about her neck in thick coils. Ryanne's breathing was uneasy.

"That is a lovely frock," he said to her, his hand slipping into hers as he walked her over to the couch. It was not a big suite, but large enough. Once she was seated, he made her a glass of ice water, more ice than water, giving it to her as he grabbed his guitar before sitting on the bed.

"I'm not thirsty," she told him.

"It is for later," he said with a grin.

Eddie leaned against the pillows as he strummed a soft tune on the guitar. A beautiful tenor voice came from lips barely moving. It was a sultry song, of a lover who was misunderstood. The more he sang, the deeper she was drawn in the words. Into him. Into this world he was creating for just the two of them to exist. He sang the last line, strummed the last chord as his eyes came up to meet hers.

Ryanne, suddenly dry mouthed, turned up the glass of water and downed it. "Was that supposed to seduce me?" she wanted to know.

"I don't know. Did it?" he asked.

"Yes. Yes it did," she said. She sat the glass on the table and moved towards him on the bed.

Eddie leaned the guitar against the side of the nightstand as he rose to meet her. Instead of embracing the body which was calling to him, he turned her around and unzipped her dress. Steady fingers pushed away the fabric and he was surprised to see she wore a slip underneath. *A good girl. Ryanne is a good girl.* He said it twice as a reminder of what type of woman he was taking to his bed.

The dress removed, he pulled the slip over her head to find a matching set of tidy white underwear. "I was wrong, Ryanne. You make these look so sexy," he said to her.

She didn't need any flashy red undies or a thong that ran a piece of floss up her butt crack. In plain white cotton undies, Eduardo was more turned on than he had been by any woman in a very long time. There was something so pure about her, even in giving herself to him, he knew she was doing it out of pain and grief. Grief that he had caused her. He could not make it right, but he could make this night for her something special.

"Eddie, I don't know why I am here really. I know I shouldn't be ..." she said to him, her hands on his chest.

"You know why you are here, Ryanne, and so do I. Even if it is just for a night, a week, a month, this is about you, about us," Eddie told her, his thumb caressing her cheek.

"Undress me, Ryanne," he commanded.

Shaky hands undid the button that was holding the shirt closed. Fingers that were also shaking slid the fabric from his shoulders as the serpent head on his chest stared at her. The red eyes almost glowed like rubies in the moonlight. She reached for his belt buckle, his arousal jutting right. *He is left handed.* She shook her head to knock away the other arbitrary thoughts that kept popping into her mind as his pants fell down around his ankles. *He is not wearing underwear.* Eddie stood before her bare, open and vulnerable.

"Look at me, Ryanne. See me as I truly am. I need for you to see me," Eduardo said. There was some other meaning in his words, which reached out to her heart.

He was beautiful. The serpent's head was only the beginning of the snake. Each scale that was etched into his skin made the snake appear to move as the tattooed serpent coiled around his body. An undigested meal sat in the middle of the snake, right above his left butt cheek, as the remainder of the snake's body wrapped around his right leg. The tail of the snake was on the top of his foot.

"I see you, Eddie," she said as she pulled the man into her arms. She held him close, feeling the warmth of his skin against her own. She repeated his words, "Even if it is just for a night, a week, a month, this is about you, about us...." She tiptoed a little so that her lips could reach his. Eduardo was hungry for companionship as his mouth devoured hers, his tongue flicking in and out of her mouth. His arms wrapped around her body, squeezing her tighter each time she exhaled. Hot lips trailed down her face to her neck as his teeth sank into the delicate skin, giving her just a nip with his teeth. She moaned as she leaned into him.

Ryanne Trodat Dobbins was an amazing woman. A nurturer. A giver. A woman with a loving heart. She was not a one-night stand. Eduardo had made a calculated risk and he was losing.

He could see himself loving Ryanne. It was something he could not afford, but it was too late. From the moment he met her, he wanted this time alone with this woman. He made love to her slowly, without hurry, as if he needed his body to remember every second in her love. She cried when she found her pleasure and he understood. He nearly cried when he found his own. The tenderness of the connection was not lost on him.

Somewhere in the middle of the night, they connected twice more, each time with the same force, the tender finish, and the missing pieces they both desired in their lives. Eduardo knew he was in trouble because Ryanne had weakened him, but there was still somethings he had to get done before he boarded his plane back to Colombia. He held her close as they slept, her legs intertwined in his own.

In her arms he felt needed.

She needed him.

This is something he would never have again unless she was a forgiving sort. He frowned in the darkness thinking about the last guy who had disappointed her. Him, she shot. In the nuts. *What would she do to me once this is all over?*

He could not afford her forgiveness, nor another night like tonight. He wanted her for himself. Even as he held her, he wanted this for himself every evening when he ended his daily tasks.

He knew it would not work, because at the end of the day, he was still a snake.

Chapter 18. Saxton ... are you drunk?

Saxton was sprawled out on the bed butt naked counting his fingers. Odessa walked into the room and he gave her a gigantic grin.

"Saxton ... have you been drinking?" she asked him. He made an attempt to sit up but plopped back down on the bed.

"Yesssss," he slurred.

He made a second attempt to sit up, failing again. This was disappointing to her because she needed to tell him about the man in the store. The uneasy feeling that had been hounding her was not going away. Ryanne's melt down along with her sudden disappearance in Lucy's Caddy did not help the matter either. She was about to talk to her father, but he'd had a couple of cups of whatever Saxton had imbibed and was stumbling from the elevator. Evidently, it was too much to try walking with his bad hip and the cane, so Big Sarge cursed out the cane, threw it on the floor, and began to crawl down the hallway. For the second time in two days, she saw her daddy cry. Each time his elbow made contact with the floor, he wailed like a frustrated toddler unable to have his way.

"Dora ... baby ... come get me," he called out like a wounded soldier on the battlefield. "I don't think I'm going to make it." His hand was held out in the air like he was reaching for the last Huey flying out of the rice patties in Nam.

"Get your drunk ass up off that floor, man, I can't carry you," Dora told him, her hands on her hips as she stood in the doorway watching him low crawl down the hall.

"You don't leave a soldier behind woman!"

"No, but I am going to leave your behind on that floor," she told him.

He rolled over to his back like a dead cockroach, his legs in the air as he held his belly. Big Sarge moaned in the air, "Dora. I love you." He passed gas, dropped his legs, and fell asleep.

Odessa called to her mother, "Mama, you need some help with him?"

Dora's hands were still on her hips. "You have your own issues to handle on that end of the hall. I had to make your naked ass husband go into his own room. He came down here wanting to talk to me ... naked! What the hell did they drink?"

She didn't know. What she did know was that her sister was out there somewhere grieving, and Saxton Blakemore was drunker than Cooter Woods on a Saturday night. He was calling her.

"Odessa! Odessa! 'Dessa ... O ... 'Dessa."

She stepped back into the room, "Yes, Saxton," she responded.

He was still playing with his fingers. "Hey, baby. When I hold my hands like this...." He forgot what he was going to say.

"Saxton ... are you drunk?" she asked just to make sure he wasn't high on something else.

"Hell yessssss, I am. Daddy had some 120 year old Scotch that was 42 proof," he said. "Wait, scratch that ... the other way around. The Scotch was 42 years old ... and 120 proof," he told her. He lay there looking at her with pride for getting it right, like he had accomplished an amazing feat.

A deep voice could be heard in the hallway, whispering, "Blakemore ... Blakemore, where you at?"

Saxton rolled to his belly on the bed, his finger and thumb aimed like a gun. "Get down, baby!" He tried to roll to sit up again and failed. "Odessa, make this damned bed stop spinning so I can cover you!"

Odessa ignored him as she opened the bedroom door. She spotted Agent Roget tiptoeing down the hall, whispering into a keyhole, "Blakemore ... you in there?"

"Agent Roget, he is over here," she said loudly.

The big man popped upright, like he had been caught red-handed, but he too was drunk and started to teeter. Odessa reached out her hand to steady him, careful to stand to the side in case he fell. She didn't want him to fall on top of her. "Are you looking for Saxton?"

"I am," he told her, trying to look dignified, but failing.

She pointed at the bed. "He's in here."

"Blakemore, we have a problem," Roget said as he wobbled across the hall. One look in the room, and the big guy started stumbling backwards. "He is nekkid! Why is he nekkid, Ms. 'Dessa? Why are you nekkid, Saxton?"

"My clothes were hot!" he yelled at Roget.

"Blakemore, I need your help, man," Roget said.

Odessa was completely over this nonsense. "Agent Roget, go to your room!" She pointed down the hall.

"That's the problem, Ms. 'Dessa. I am lost. I don't know where the hell my room is ... this is a big ass house," he told her as he looked over her shoulder at Saxton. His eyes got wide as he yelled at his friend. "Man, cut that out!"

Odessa turned to find Saxton with little Saxton in his hand.

He picked it up and it flopped.

He picked it up and it flopped again.

He grabbed at it one more time, a scared look covering his face. "Odessa, I think he is drunk, too! He may need mouth to mouth to resuscitate him!" He told her with an uncharacteristic giggle.

"Oh My Ghhherrrrrrrrd!" she exclaimed as she spotted Belva come up the stairs. Odessa held up her hands to stop his sister from coming into the room. "Saxton is naked and playing with himself."

Belva only shrugged. "Well, some things never change." She looked down the hall to see Big Sarge sleeping on the floor. "I should have known they had gotten into the Scotch when Uncle Dusty came into the baby shower with his boots off, wiggling that deformed big toe at the ladies."

Roget spoke up. "Yeah, what was up with that? His toe looked like a deformed penis."

Belva sighed as she looked at Roget, trying to hold up the wall. She told Odessa, "I got this. Come on with me, big guy." She put her arm around the agent and helped him the other side of the hall. "You are staying in my wing."

Agent Roget didn't care. He had been staring at Saxton's sister since he arrived. She was a very attractive woman. "You're pretty," he told her. "You smell like flowers covered in dew on a fairies nose."

"That's nice," she said. Belva guided him past the stairs. "So, Marecus ... is that an African name?"

"Why do y'all white folks keep asking me that?" he said as she aided him into a room.

Saxton was splayed out on the bed. At least he didn't

still have his junk in his hands. He'd somehow managed to roll over twice and show her his bum. "Odessa, is my ass still there? I can't feel it...."

This was all too much. She decided instead of taking a chance with her drunk husband, she would go and sleep in the room Ryanne was in. At least when her sister came back, they could talk.

Ryanne's room wasn't empty. Instead, she found her brother resting there. Face down in the bed. Also butt naked.

"Oh My Ghhherrrrrrrrd!" she yelled.

This was insane. But Thanksgiving was about to get worse.

It was going to get a hell of a lot worse.

Chapter 19. Say what now…?

Victorío arrived on Thanksgiving morning to find a table full of hung over men. Well, everyone but Dusty and Bobby Ray. Those two were bright-eyed, bushy-tailed, and getting the fires started for roasting the pig in the pit. Dusty stood by the fire, using a long hot poker to dig in the coals, mix in the wood chips along with mesquite chunks to get the fire ready for the meat. Another grill was fired up for ribs so that Bobby Ray could show off to his new best buddy, Big Sarge, his famous bar-be que sauce.

Unfortunately, after spending much of the night on the hallway floor, Big Sarge was not only hungover, but stiff, sore, and bordering on cranky. Lucy had the cure all as she doled out her hangover remedy and passed everyone a glass. She stopped in front of her eldest son, staring at him.

"Saxton, it is good to see you this morning with clothes on. I don't know why you decided to come find me in the middle of the night to talk about the meaning of life, butt raving naked," she told him.

Saxton only mumbled under his breath. "My clothes were hot."

There were many other items on Lucy's mind to discuss with her son. At the top of the list were all the bullet holes in his body. Tears flooded her eyes when he walked away from her last night and guilt took over. *Had I been a better mother, he would have never run off into danger to prove himself.* This morning, a new feeling had taken over Lucy, and along with the celebration of the holiday, there were many things for which to be thankful. Her son was home and she was going to be a grandmother.

Odessa was past grateful when Ryanne walked through the back door around 9:30 am. It was obvious to all that the Ryanne who walked through the door in the morning was not the one who walked out last night. The version that came through the doorway for breakfast was full of spark, seemed sated, and was carrying a great deal of confidence – confidence that shone through when a call came in from Dwight's mother.

Ryanne took the call at the kitchen table as she ate like a woman who had not seen food in a month. "I'm sorry, Mrs. Dobbins, but I am not in Corpus Christie. I am in Houston. I have been in Houston since Monday."

There were questions flung at her along with accusations through the phone. "I did not kill your son. Yes, I shot him, but I didn't kill him."

Screaming could be heard through the line. "You want answers about his death? Start with his bank accounts. Whomever was paying him all that extra money is who you have a fight with, not me," she told her very upset mother-in-law.

"No, that is not true, Mrs. Dobbins. I found out about the bribes at 3:30 in the morning from a phone call he was having in the kitchen. When I would not play along is when he decided to beat me into acceptance. I will tell you the same thing I told him, my father doesn't hit me, and neither would he ... which is why I shot him," Ryanne told her.

Mrs. Dobbins was still yelling. "I'm sorry your son is dead but whomever was paying him is probably who killed him.... No, not necessary. I will have the body released to you as well as everything in his bank accounts. I will have my things out of the house by Saturday and I want nothing else to do with him."

Dwight's mother was still talking when Ryanne hung up the phone. She looked around the table. "Can someone pass me those grits?"

She was smiling as she guzzled down a glass of orange juice. "I am so thirsty this morning!"

Renteria was deep in a conversation with Connard about airplanes, when Odessa spoke to her husband.

"Saxton, the oddest thing happened yesterday in the mercantile," she started to say to her husband. "This man took a selfie with me. He took one with Ms. Patsy as well ... wait," she said. Odessa darted up the stairs, or as fast as she could move with a small bowling ball for a belly. She returned a few minutes later with her phone. "I took a selfie with him too."

Odessa turned the phone to Saxton. "Have you ever seen this guy before? He said his name was Eddie."

Ryanne's head came up slowly. *How does she know Eddie?*

The phone was floating about the table as others took a peek. Saxton, who could almost hear a rat urinate on cotton, was having trouble drowning out ambient sounds. Everything sounded loud to him. Especially when Renteria came into the room, saw the selfie, and dropped his glass.

"*Ay Dios Mio*! Do you know who that is?" he asked.

Everyone, including Ryanne, all asked, "Who is he?"

Renteria legs were giving way under him as he fumbled to get to a chair, trying to sit while talking at the same time. "That is Eduardo Delgado! The head of the Zeta Cartel! He is Hugo's younger brother and the man who sent Mateo to kill you."

Saxton was stone cold sober now. He sat up alert and staring at the photo. *I have not been paying attention. I let my guard down and he got this close to my wife and son.*

Ryanne remained quiet. Big Sarge could not. "He doesn't seem like that big of a bad ass to me. That Mateo guy was more intimidating than this dude."

"Well, Mateo is dead. This dude ..." Renteria paused. He pointed at the pic of the man in the phone, "... sent me Mateo's head in a box yesterday."

"Say what now?" Ryanne asked. It was all too much for her, as she tried to stand, lost her footing, which caused her plate to flip off the table, a plate that also served as a receptacle for the vomit that also flowed from her mouth. Dora was trying to console her as shots could be heard in the distance.

"Where is Roget?" Saxton asked.

"Where is Kevin?" Odessa wanted to know.

"Where did the shots come from?" Renteria asked.

Dusty came into the kitchen. "The shots came from the stables."

"Odessa, ladies, you stay here. Grandma, arm the women folk, we will be back in a jiffy," Saxton said as he darted out the back door, each footfall reminding him of his pounding head.

It was indeed a beautiful horse. As a lover of horse flesh and all things fine, Eduardo appreciated the regal bearing of the black stallion. His intention had been to simply take a photo with the animal. Longshot was not having any part of it. As Eduardo leaned against the stall, the horse clamped down on his shoulder and bit him. "You son of a bi-..." Eduardo swore at the beast.

Longshot had learned early how to open his stall. This was also a surprise for Eduardo when the horse bent his head, lifted the latch, and came out of the stall at him. All Eduardo could see was black muscle coming at him with hooves, teeth, and anger. His hands were up defensively when Roget came into the stables.

"What in the hell?" Roget asked. When Eduardo turned, Roget knew immediately who he was. "How the fu-..." was all Roget managed to get out, as Eduardo pulled his gun and flipped off the safety, firing three shots.

One was a warning to the horse, who did not slowdown in his attack. The second went into the horse's head and third one went into Roget's leg. The big man dropped. The blood was spurting from his leg as Eduardo looked at him, raised his gun in the air, and fired another shot. The horses went into a tizzy as he heard footsteps coming his way in a hurry. Eduardo opened the doors of the rear stalls, setting those horses free. He made a point of steering them away from Roget as he ran out the back entrance using the horses as cover.

Roget was losing a lot of blood and Longshot was dead. And that was only the start of Thanksgiving Day.

Chapter 20. Call 911 …

Saxton arrived in the barn to find Roget bleeding out. At that rate, he was not going to survive until the ambulance arrived. Everyone in the barn knew it, but Saxton was home, he wasn't in the field. On the ranch, there was nothing his daddy couldn't fix and make better. He yelled at the top of his lungs, "Daddy! Help!"

Bobby Ray had made it to the barn when he saw Marecus on the ground and all the blood. "Holy shit balls, they got an artery!"

Without saying a word, Bobby Ray turned and took off running. Dusty was in the barn locating a piece of leather to tie off Roget's leg. The hot poker that was jutting out of the pit, Bobby Ray pulled, turned on his boot heel, and started running again for the stables. At 65 years old, the patriarch was in great condition. At 6'3, a solid 225 pounds, it was impressive to see the grey-haired version of Saxton moving so deftly. It was uncertain how smart it was to run with a red-hot poker in his hands, but a life was at stake.

Winded, but focused, he said, "Hold him down!" Dusty had already torn away Roget's pants leg as the hot poker sizzled as it made contact with flesh.

Saxton's gloved hand had been inserted into Roget's mouth for the man to bite down on while Bobby Ray cauterized the bleeder. The agent's limp body was cradled in Saxton's arms. Saxton refused to let anyone touch Marecus until the ambulance came. Roget's dark skin had taken on an ashen hue as everyone stood around waiting for the ambulance to arrive.

"Saxton," Bobby Ray spoke softly. "I stopped the

bleeding, but he has lost a lot of blood."

"I'm O negative, we can transfuse him here, just pump some of my blood into him, Daddy!" Saxton's insistent voice made Bobby Ray want to try, but he didn't. He watched with interest the visual of his son cradling the fallen agent. It was obvious the love his son had for his friend.

"I think I got that vein sealed up in time son, we just have to wait," he told him.

"He's my friend, Daddy. He is a good friend. I can't let him die on my watch," Saxton insisted. His eyes were full of tears as he looked over at Longshot. He wasn't certain if he was crying for his horse, his friend, or for allowing the enemy inside of the gates. *Eduardo was standing next to my wife. That bastard was posing with her and my grandmother.*

"Don't you die on me, Roget! If you die, I am going to be really pissed at you!" Saxton yelled at the limp body that he was cradling in his arms. His emotions were overtaking him, unraveling him at his core.

Bobby Ray spoke to his son. "I know you are his friend, son, but what he needs right now is for you to be the agent in charge. You need to go to work, Agent Blakemore," Bobby Ray said.

Agent Blakemore was back at work. He used his father's phone to call into the office. The ambulance arrived alongside a special detail to keep Roget secure as he was transported to the hospital. The stables were locked down. Dusty and the crew gathered up Longshot's remains as Saxton tried hard not to look at the horse as it was taken away. *What kind of man kills a horse? A sadistic one that's going to die a horrible, painful death.*

Inside the house, the women were fretful as Saxton walked in covered in blood. Ryanne's face was grey as she looked at all the blood on her brother-in-law.

"Saxton?" Odessa asked with the lightest of voices.

"I don't know yet. Daddy cauterized the bleed, but we don't know. Eduardo shot Roget and nicked an artery," his voice was brimming with emotion. "He also killed Longshot." The collective gasps almost sucked all the air from the room.

Ryanne's phone rang and it was Eduardo's face on the screen. Saxton looked at her in confusion. She answered the phone, "Hello?"

"Please put me on speaker, Mrs. Dobbins," Eduardo said into her ear. He was not using the American accent.

With a few swipes of her finger, she placed the phone on speaker as her late night lover came over the line. "Good morning, Blakemores. It seems that on this Thursday American holiday, you have a great deal for which to be thankful."

Saxton was furious. "You should be thankful that I didn't get to that barn in time."

Eduardo clucked into the phone. "I do admit, Agent Blakemore, I thought you would be far more formidable. It has been a bit of a disappointment. You have offered me no real challenge."

"So you took it out on my horse instead?" Saxton asked.

"And your wife killed my brother!" Eduardo exclaimed.

"But that was a magnificent and good horse," Saxton responded. The line was quiet. Eduardo exhaled.

"I want and need you to understand, Blakemore, that I have touched everything near and dear to you. I can get close any time I want to and take away everything that makes you stand upright," Eduardo said.

That weird feeling that had been bothering Odessa was back. "Kevin ... where is my brother?"

Eduardo laughed. "He is in the barn. He is unhurt."

Saxton was beyond furious. "You come into my home, touch my family, and you expect me to do nothing?"

The cartel leader raised his voice. "You will not do a goddamned thing! You should be very thankful today that the only thing I did kill was your fucking horse!"

The line was quiet. Eduardo was tired of all of them. "You stay away from me and my operations and I will stay away from you. If you make one move towards anything I own and operate, next time it will not be your favorite animal."

He clicked off the line.

The family stood stunned.

Lucy was the first to speak. "Sobriety is grossly overrated. I need a damned drink! Somebody bring me a frickin' highball!"

Chapter 21. Dinner with the Blakemores

It was the longest Thanksgiving in history. Saxton showered, removing all the blood from him as he took his truck into town to check on Roget. It was an unsettling experience for everyone, especially Ryanne. The confusion she was feeling was palpable. Eduardo had not made mention of their night together, or how they had met, or even how he had her number.

Her father wanted to know, as well as everyone else. "How did you meet him, Odessa?" Ryanne asked, changing the subject and getting the heat off of her.

"I met him in the mercantile when I went in the store with Ms. Patsy. He said he was a traveling musician and wanted to take a photo with me for his kids. He said he wanted to show them all the nice people he was meeting while he was on tour in Texas," she said.

"Where did you meet him, Ryanne?" Big Sarge wanted to know. Dora already knew the answer, as well as where her daughter was last night and whom she was with.

"I met him a few days ago. He told me the same thing and he took a picture with me. He took a selfie with me on my phone," she told them. She swiped back through her phone to photos before the baby shower to show them. "He sent this selfie to himself. I guess that is how he got my number."

Big Sarge bought it, Odessa bought it, but Dora knew better. The look her daughter had on her face when she walked through that door was the look of a woman who spent the night being made love to. It was more interesting to Dora that Eduardo Delgado made no mention of it during his call. The cartel leader was very careful in his word choice. He'd told Saxton, *I have touched everything near and dear to you*; Dora knew that included her daughter.

The question that plagued Dora was why Ryanne had also chosen her words so carefully. She had done it on the phone with Dwight's mother and she was doing it now. The pieces were there and Dora was seeing the whole puzzle. "Do you think that this man could have also killed Dwight, Ryanne?"

Dora watched her daughter give the first honest answer out of her mouth since she walked in that door. "I don't know, Mama. He could have been the man paying Dwight for information on us."

Ryanne was torn. What she felt last night with Eddie was real. *I know it was real. It had to have been real to him as well because he didn't mention it.* She knew he could have humiliated her in front of her family but he didn't. Kevin was not so lucky.

He had tied him up as he found him sleeping. Something that did not go unnoticed by anyone, especially the Blakemores. Eduardo had gotten into their home and taken a drugged up Kevin out of his room. A chill ran across Odessa as she wondered if he had been in the room with Kevin when she had gone in to check on her brother last night before she went to bed.

Ryanne could not speak up, because pointing out that Eduardo must have had an inside man to get Kevin out of his bed and out of the house would raise too many questions. She knew Eduardo didn't take Kevin out of the house last night. The man could not be in two places at once. As active as he was in bed with her, she was surprised he even had the energy to do everything he'd done today. She barely had any energy herself.

Dora was watching her closely. "Baby, maybe a hot shower will help you feel better."

Again she was torn. The smell of Eduardo was still on her skin. Washing her body would be like washing away the best memory she would have of this whole dark scenario. "Actually, Mama, I feel better than I have felt in a very long time." Even after throwing up her breakfast, she understood that her time with Eduardo Delgado was far from over.

A man like that never leaves a stone unturned. He had removed her from the equation for a reason; for what purpose she was uncertain. The thing she was certain about was that nothing he did was random.

He even made love with a purpose.

By the time dinner rolled around, Lucy Blakemore was drunk, Bobby Ray was furious, and Connard wanted to be anywhere but at another family function. He sat in the kitchen at the table listening to another one of his mother's drunken speeches about the importance of family and sticking together. He'd had enough.

"Oh shut up, Mama!" He said it out loud.

Every head at the gigantic dinner table turned to look at him. "I am so sick of the bullshit and fake platitudes. You are a drunk and I am sending you to rehab. For God's sake, you are about to be a grandmother. No one is going to trust some drunk, dull-brained woman with their child!"

Lucy's mouth was flopping open and shut like she was gasping for air. Connard kept going. "Go ahead and get sauced today, because tomorrow, the men in the white truck are coming for you!"

Bobby Ray sprang to his feet. "Son, you have no right!"

"I have every right, Daddy. I am the head of Blakemore Oil and it is my responsibility to make sure the company moves forward. I want to make sure this family moves forward as well. We hide behind our words when we should be looking at our actions. And I am taking some action. I am also getting a divorce," he said. "I have worked out a settlement with her, and she is officially out of my life."

Dusty spoke up, "So does this mean you are finally bringing your happy ass out of the closet?"

"I am kicking down the damn closet door," Connard explained. He looked at Lucy. "And, yes, all of your socialite friends are going to find out the two of you have a gay son!"

Big Sarge and Dora were watching the action go back and forth down the table. Dora's eyes were affixed on Lucy. Big Sarge was focused in on Bobby Ray, who stood, lifted his wine glass in askance for a toast. "I will make a toast and I want to go around the table and have each of you state the thing that you are most thankful to have."

Connard was confused.

This was not the reaction he was expecting from his father.

Big Sarge went first. He was thankful for his children and loving wife.

Ryanne spoke. "I am thankful for finally finding my voice."

Kevin, who had been very quiet the entire day, spoke softly. "I am thankful whoever kidnapped me last night didn't pull a *Pulp Fiction* on me." He looked at Odessa, mouthing the words, *"Why was I naked?"*

His sister, whose hand rubbed her belly, said, "I am thankful for all of you, my husband, and this little guy."

Dora was thankful for her family. Belva was grateful for fresh starts. Uncle Dusty, well, when he finished, no one was certain what he was talking about. Neither was his wife, his two sons, or his grandkids at the kiddie table in the kitchen.

Grandma Patsy had nothing to say. She was still trying to understand why she was still alive. This was the worst Thanksgiving dinner in her family history. The dinner table looked like an ad for a diversity poster.

Lucy, still stunned, picked up the bottle of Chardonnay, threw it against the wall and started yelling for someone to bring her a frickin' highball.

Saxton, who recently came through the door, brought good news. "Roget pulled through." He picked up his glass from the table sidestepping the broken wine bottle, acting as if he didn't even see his mother's outburst. This was also something that everyone in Odessa's family noticed as he picked up his glass to make his toast. "I am very grateful to my father, his quick thinking, and always being there whenever I needed him. In your honor, Odessa and I would like to show our gratitude to you by naming our son Robert Raymond Blakemore, III."

Bobby Ray's eyes teared up. He used the back of his massive, age-weathered hands to wipe away the tears as he stood and said, "Raise your glasses. I am grateful for my family." He looked down the table, making eye contact with everyone seated. "You have reminded me this week how important family is. And to you, Connard, thank you for making the decision to do something I never could; get your damned mama sober."

"And my life choice, Daddy? Will you still love me ... and not disown me?"

Bobby Ray moved around the table so fast, everyone was scared to move. He pulled Connard into his arms. "I have loved you unconditionally from the first time I held you in my arms. I will love you unconditionally to the last time I can hold you in my arms."

Big Sarge sat up. "This is better than watching a soap opera, but damn it, I'm hungry and I have to take my pill. Can we eat?"

Chapter 22. Still reeling …

Friday, Dallas, TX

The flight back to Dallas was quiet as Big Sarge tried to understand everything that had occurred during the week. It was shocking to learn that his grandbaby was going to inherit the Blakemore kingdom. An even more pleasant surprise was how well Odessa was handling it all. Hell, he was shocked how well Ryanne was dealing with the craziness that struck her out of left field. She had only been married six months and was a widow.

Dora walked into the den to find him staring out the window. "Honey, are you okay?"

"I am. There was just so much to process," he told her. His hip was bothering him more each day and sleeping on the floor had not helped.

"I'm still reeling from so much happening. What bothers me more than anything is that someone walked into that house, picked our son up out of bed, and carried him to the barn. Someone was in their house, baby!" Dora told him with surprise on her face.

Big Sarge still had not moved. "Life is so fleeting. I am thankful whoever it was didn't want our boy dead. I am also grateful they didn't take Bobby Ray's boy either, he loves his son. I have come to love Saxton as well."

Dora was watching him. She wanted her husband to say what she was thinking. "And what about Ryanne?"

He turned a bit to face her. "She is about to undergo some changes as she finds herself. I knew so many years of schooling would make her miss too much. Now she is going to try and capture a new kind of life, because she has never had one outside of a classroom."

"What about the Eduardo guy?" Dora asked.

Big Sarge was now completely facing his wife. In his right hand he held his cane, in the left, he held up a bottle of the 42-year-old Scotch that Bobby Ray had given him. "It is going to have to run its course, Dora. I didn't miss it either. She is the reason why Kevin is not dead. Something happened between them...but that Eduardo fellow didn't want her put on blast about it. The rest ... I'm not going to think about right now."

In an effort to change the subject, Dora went in from the left side of the conversation. "Saxton's family was nice. Can you believe his grandmother gave the baby an oil well?"

Big Sarge chuffed. "Yeah, it will probably be spitting out the same thing Old Patsy does – dust!"

He moved to the counter to grab two glasses. "You know this stuff is a thousand dollars a bottle. Bobby Ray gave me a case," he said to Dora. He poured a finger of Scotch for him and his wife, taking a seat on the couch beside her. "I am blessed to be alive and see my children become adults. In a little while we will be proud grandparents."

"Yes, but that child will have to call me Gigi or something. I am way too sexy to be anyone's grandma!" Dora told him.

"You got that right," Big Sarge said as he pulled his wife in for a kiss.

Friday night, Dallas, TX

Saxton was leaning back in the tub, squeezing his

favorite rubber duck, Plucky, his mind whirling with thoughts and ideas, but most of all the realization that they had come close to dying again. His mind was made up. He was quitting the agency. Uncle Dusty would be 65 the following year and ready to retire. He and his wife lived in the ranch house on site and completed many upgrades to the old house. The ranch had always been the only thing he wanted to run, never the company. Connard could keep that job. He would ask him to train his son to succeed him, but that, too, would be up to Connard.

"Mr. Blakemore, it's time for bed," Odessa called to him.

He flipped the drain plug to release the water from the tub. The housekeeper comes in tomorrow, but he never liked leaving a dirty tub. He dried off quickly before entering the bedroom.

"Can't sleep without all of this sexy, can you?" he asked.

"You know it is hard for me," she told him.

Saxton stuck his hand underneath the towel. "Not yet, but I can make it happen for you, baby."

She laughed at his innuendo. "Yes, but we know that can't happen when you are drunk."

"Yeah ... about that ..." he said sheepishly as he climbed into bed with her.

Odessa placed her finger to his lips. "We don't need to talk about that, or mention it, ever ... ever ... ever again."

He laughed as he pulled her close. "We do need to talk about Eduardo and him killing my horse...."

She rolled over to face him. "In all honesty, you can buy another horse. I cannot buy another sister or brother. He could have done to them what he did to Mateo."

"Do you think that is where Ryanne was Wednesday night; with Eduardo... he specifically said he touched everything close to me..." Saxton asked.

"I don't want or need to speak about that ever again either. If she were with Eduardo on Wednesday night, it means that he didn't personally come in that house to take out Kevin, but someone on your parents' staff is on his payroll," she told her husband.

Saxton nodded. "I did pull Dwight's bank accounts. He was on someone's payroll as well, just like she said."

"Hubby, I want a normal life for our son... our children," she told him.

"There is no such thing as normal. In either of my worlds. In the spy world, people want to kill me. In the Blakemore world, people kiss my ass because of my name. I hate them both, but at least when I take over the ranch, it can be as normal as we make it," he told her.

"You seem excited about taking it over. Moving our import company won't be too hard," she told him.

He was grinning at her lasciviously. "Hmmm... Odessa..."

Odessa put her finger over his lips. "Say goodnight, Mr. Blakemore."

"Goodnight," he said.

Friday night, Dallas, TX

Ryanne stepped from the bath holding the oversized towel around her body. The steam from the shower had fogged up the mirror and she could barely see her reflection. She used an end of the towel to wipe away some of the condensation as she stared at the image of herself that gazed back at the new woman she had morphed into. As she regarded herself in the mirror, she noticed the teeth marks on her collarbone. *He sank those fangs into my skin.*

Using her finger, she traced over the indentations of Eddie's teeth in her flesh. Her hand moved down to the brown skin which covered her breast. The perfect shape of that man's mouth left marks upon her skin where he had pressed his lips together while he sucked at her flesh, creating small hematomas. They were also on the insides of her thighs, and one on her right butt cheek.

"I am 34 years old and covered in hickeys," she said to herself. She turned in the mirror to check her back. It was covered in scratches that looked like claw marks. So much of her life had been spent in a classroom, educating herself via books. In one night, Eddie, Eduardo, or whatever his name was, had schooled her in the ways of love. He was only the third man she had ever been intimate with and if she had her way, he would easily be her last.

The pleasure he brought to her body as she surrender herself to their passion was earth shattering. The mere thought of his mouth on her breast, rushed blood to the capillaries drawing the skin around the buds tight.

"Damn it Eddie!" She said as she heard her phone chime in the other room. She moved to the dresser to see his face on the screen. Her initial response was to run her fingers across the image of his lips before swiping the screen to answer the call.

"Hello," she said.

She heard his voice catch as he exhaled in relief. Eduardo spoke in the phone in a breathy voice, "I know you are thinking about me because I can't stop thinking about you."

"This is not a good idea," she told him.

"I don't care. I want...no I need to see you again," he said.

"That is a worse idea," she told him.

The line was quiet as the lover's waited for the other to state the next words. Ryanne was saying nothing, but Eduardo had a lot to say.

"Ryanne, if you felt nothing from the night we shared, I will hang up and say no more," Eduardo told her.

She hated herself for wanting him, but she did. She spoke the words she knew he wanted to hear, "Even if it is just for a night... this is about you, about us...."

Eduardo's smile was almost audible through the phone, "I will come to you when it is safe."

And he hung up.

Ryanne knew he was dangerous. Dangerous in the worst kind of way, but the way he made love to her, she didn't care. Even if it was just once more...she was going to go for it.

I deserve some happiness too.

Chapter 23. And how did we get here …

Sunday Morning, Dallas, TX

Ryanne stood at the kitchen sink in her parent's home. Technically, it was her home, too, or at least it would be until she could figure out what to do next with her life. The meeting with Dwight's parents yesterday was not as stressful as she had imagined. When she met his parents at the bank, there was close to two million dollars in his account, something which shocked the Dobbins. Ryanne signed it over to them, along with the house, his vehicle, and any assets he owned. Always a bit of a minimalist, she had not collected a vast amount of anything, including clothes, shoes, or handbags. What she owned in that house equaled four boxes that shipped home via UPS.

His mother was in tears. His father didn't seem too surprised by anything that had transpired, or if he did, he said very little. "I'm sorry for the loss of your son." That was all she had to give them. The past three months, she had given Dwight even less. It had been almost that long since they'd slept together, and most of her time was spent at work. A job that she truly had grown to despise. She sent her official resignation via email with a newspaper clipping of her husband's death. That was all she had to give to them as well.

The ice tea glass she had in her hands held a smudge of her mother's greasy lipstick that didn't seem to want to come off, no matter how much she scrubbed. Ryanne looked up and out the window to see Eduardo standing in the back yard looking back at her. The glass crumpled in her hand, cutting the flesh, leaving little shards of glass imbedded in the skin.

"Shit! Shit! Shit!" she exclaimed as she tried to rinse away some of the blood. She looked out the window again and he was not there. The back door knob turned and he let himself inside of the house.

His concern was for her hand as he immediately rushed to her side to care for her injury. Ryanne was jolted by how easily he had gotten into the house.

"You do know that if my daddy catches you here, he will shoot you?" she told him.

In a heavy South American accent, he responded, "I am more concerned about you shooting me."

"Where did that accent come from? When you spoke to me before there was no accent ..." she cried.

"I don't have an accent. Everyone in my country sounds like this," he told her, his index finger running across her skin, checking for remaining shards. He looked into her eyes as he switched back to his perfect Texas accent. "Does this help? I mean to sound more North American?"

She shook her head. "That whole Colombian accent thing is working for you. I would stick with that one."

Eduardo cleaned the cut and blotted at the skin with a paper towel. "You should add some ointment to it, so that it does not get infected." He bandaged her hand with extra napkins and sat down at the kitchen table. He sat there as boldly as if he had been invited in for coffee.

Since she had just brewed a pot, she poured him a cup, as well as one for herself, and took a seat at the table next to him. *This is too frickin' weird.* "Did you come to have sex with me before killing me and leaving the country?" *I said it. It's out.*

The look on his face registered genuine shock. "I am not

some psycho! Why would I kill *you*?"

"Well, you did kill Saxton's horse," she told him. "And that Mateo guy ... you put his head in a box...."

Eduardo sighed deeply. "Good God, *Carina*! Your sister killed my brother. I killed a damned horse. I mean, if this were to actually be even, I can still kill your brother!"

She held up her hands defensively. "No, not necessary," she told him. "*Carina*?" She asked sheepishly.

"Uhmm, loosely translated, it means sweetheart," he said as he noticed her hand. The right one had started to bleed again. "Let me see that," he told her. Eduardo unwrapped the paper towels to check the cuts again. As if he lived in the house, he went to the fridge, located a stick of butter, cut off a pat and rubbed it across the cuts. The butter picked up a few extra shards that he had missed. He rewrapped her hand and placed a small kiss in the palm. "Now ... it is all better."

"Thanks," she said. It confused the hell out of her how he managed to know the perfect time to show up. He was sitting in the kitchen as if it were a normal day in their lives.

"Eduardo ..." she started.

"No ... for you ... you call me Eddie," he said. His dark eyes were looking for something in her face. Ryanne was uncertain of what he sought, so she asked.

"Eddie, honestly why are you here?"

"You know, I am asking myself the same damned thing. I should have went with my first option, and this uncomfortable space between us would be no more," he said with an eerie calmness.

"What was your first option, if I may ask?" she truly wanted to know.

His eyebrows were up in a mock surprise. "I was going to drug you, throw you over my shoulder and take you back to my country ... but I didn't think you would appreciate that choice."

Ryanne did not move. Neither did her face. "Your option sounds a great deal like kidnapping!"

Eduardo grinned as he gnawed on his bottom lip, "You North Americans and all of your techie terms. I am just saying I was considering it as a viable option..."

Her expression had not changed, "And how and why was that an option to anyone but you?"

He shrugged. "It sure as hell beats having this conversation."

Her eyes finally managed to blink. "What conversation?" She needed a new approach. Evidently so did he, as he sipped at the coffee. He spat it out.

"What is this swill that I am drinking?" he asked.

Ryanne got up to pull the coffee canister from the cabinet. "It says it is a Colombian roast."

"That is not Colombian coffee. You come to my country, I make you a great cup of coffee that you will write home and tell your parents about...it is so good."

The silence between them was thick. She needed to know the truth. "Eddie, did you kill my husband to get to me?"

Eduardo understood the question; he simply didn't know how to answer it. Or at least the answer he had would not be the right one, so he tried to play it off. "I don't understand this question you ask of me."

"Oh, now you want to have a language barrier?"

"Again, you North Americans and your sayings. It is so

confusing at times. I'm sorry, I do not understand." He was smiling when he said it. He also made the Colombian accent thicker on purpose.

"Fine. Did you kill my husband so you could have me?" she asked flatly.

The smile left his face. Eduardo leaned forward and rubbed his index finger across the fine hairs on her arm. "From the moment I laid eyes on you in that store, buying those ridiculous packages of white cotton undies, I knew I would have you."

It was so raw, so passionate, and so intense, that Ryanne had to cross her legs. She uncrossed them at his next words. "Your husband, I killed because he was a lying, manipulative asshole. His instructions were to get you the job, date you, and keep an eye on the family. He married you and took out a large insurance policy... He was going to kill you and cash in...I did not sanction that...nor his actions. He also put his hands on you and bruised this beautiful face."

Ryanne's eyes closed as she gave in to his seductive touch. "I feel what you feel, and appreciate the chances you are taking coming here, Eddie. I just don't know if I can go through with this...it is too damned weird and wrong."

His words were soft as he caressed her cheek. "I could not leave without holding you one more time. I need to feel your lips upon mine before you exhale your breath in my ear when I connect our bodies. I want to move in the intimate dance of love with you, feeling the sweetness of you wrapped around me, pulling me in, telling me that in the end, what matters is us...Ryanne, what happened between us was real ... I couldn't leave without asking you to ..."

"Asking me to what?"

His next words stole her breath. "I am asking you to... hell, I don't know what I am asking anymore, but I was hoping that you could see the man...and maybe visualize yourself loving him."

She was genuinely surprised. "And how did we get here?"

"We got here by me letting down my guard for a night and allowing you into my inner sanctum. You slipped in and I can't get you out of my thoughts, my head, my heart.... I haven't felt this way in a very long time about anyone ... or anything, Ryanne. I feel so much when I am with you. Come home with me. Let me show you my country ... my world..."

She was shaking her head. "But you are the leader of a Colombian drug cartel."

"No, I am a farmer," he told her.

Her lips were tight. "And what do you grow on this farm?"

Eduardo shrugged his shoulders. "Coca and coffee."

"Coca, as in the plant from which cocaine is extracted?"

He smiled at her. "Yes. It is how I make my living. Not everyone has a choice in professions, Ryanne. Inside of this body, I am just a man with a job. Each night I go to bed alone. It is a lonely life. I am asking for you to spend some time with me ... let me take you on a date...maybe sail around Cape Horn..."

She said nothing.

He threw up his hands and stood. "See! This is why I was truly considering option 1," he told her.

"I understand what you are asking, Eddie, and I see

you," she said. "I have a lot of loose ends to tie up here. Maybe ... I don't know...in a month or so I could possibly come for a week."

"I hope I did not disappoint you as a lover," he asked with a face full of concern.

"Oh, no. You were ... um ... exceptional, I was very happy. Several times. That ... oh crap," she said giving in to the heat of him standing so close to her. "Honestly, Eddie, after that performance, I didn't see how you had the energy to kill a horse, shoot a man, and scatter the livestock...."

He rubbed his chest massaging the spot where Longshot had kicked him. "I was tired as hell, I tell you that...."

Eduardo shuddered as he paused while a thought struck him, "And why does your brother sleep naked in November? He should understand that if a fire were to break out he would have to leave the house without wearing any clothing!"

She could not help it. She started to giggle. The whole conversation was so over the top ridiculous that she had to laugh at it all.

Eduardo checked his watch. "We are almost out of time. Your parents will be home in a half hour."

"How do you know that?"

"Really, Ryanne?" His eyebrows were up again. "I have an idea on how I would like to spend our last moments before I leave your country ... just a few minutes that are about us."

Why the hell not? I deserve some happiness, too. Even if it is only for a half hour. "A half hour ..."

"I can make a lot happen in ten minutes. If you are nice,

I can take you there twice in twenty," he grinned.

She held up her good hand. "I will be as sweet as sugar in the cane," she said as he pulled her up from the chair, threw her over his shoulder, and headed down the hallway. Ryanne was giggling like a school girl.

One last time with him...with my Eddie.

It may not have been an ideal match or a perfect ending, but Eduardo did not think his trip to North America was in vain. There would be others he had to answer to for not killing the Blakemores, but he would deal with that when the time came. In his mind, he had accomplished what he set out to do, and in the middle of all the chaos, he found a woman who spoke to his heart.

That, he was certain, was not by a random chance.

-Fin –

Olivia Gaines

The Blakemore Files, Book 6

THE COST to Play

Two Cosplayers set out to create the perfect comic book, but find that they are also perfect for each other.

Olivia Gaines

Chapter 1 -

There are some daybreaks when a body awakens and is ready for the day to commence. It was going to be one of those mornings when a girl felt like she had just stepped into a scene in a Disney movie. The day would begin with that perfect quaint scene in the movie where blue birds fluttered about, flowers bloomed as the pretty girl walked by, and a tune filled the lungs exhibiting how great a girl was feeling. Jayne Wright's mood was just that good as she parked her Chevy Equinox on the street. Today, nothing could dampen her spirit. She began to sing as she made her way to the office. She bobbed her head to the left, swayed her hips to the right, and moved her shoulders to an imaginary beat as she belted out a few notes to an old R & B song. This day could not be more perfect.

"Yo baby! You lucky you got an ass like that. It almost makes up for your singing and dancing," said some man rolling by in a wheelchair on the sidewalk. Jayne gulped as if she had just swallowed a very large bug. The old fart didn't even bother to look back as he continued to roll down the sidewalk, now singing the same song, but in tune and in key. Even Wheelchair Willie's snarky comment was not going to ruin her day.

Friends often mocked her for giving every person a funny moniker, but it was her thing. It did not matter to Jayne in the least about whether she met with other's expectations of her. It was irrelevant. She was her own person, with her own mind, and her own way of doing things. Her Grandma Pearl often chided her mother, "that's what you get for naming a black Chile Jayne." She liked her name and the person she had grown up to be. Independent, free thinking, and a very talented artist.

Unfortunately her talent on paper did not translate to her abilities with humans. It was even worse when it came to humans of the opposite sex. Her inability to understand and relate to men who wanted her as an arm piece befuddled her mind. It was almost a rude shock to her existence when a man would take her to dinner and make bumbling attempts to have her for dessert. Jayne LaQueeda Wright was not that type of woman. Most days, she wasn't sure what type of woman she was exactly, but it wasn't one that was easy.

Simplicity, however, was how she lived her life. Cawley Public Relations had been her first real job out of college and five years later she was still there. Serving as the lead designer and project manager, her work was on billboards all over Augusta, Georgia. Grandma Pearl even swore she saw an ad in Atlanta as well. It was humorous to her, even though she tried several times to explain it to her Grammy, only a handful of their clients were local. When she returned home one evening with her Clio award, Grandma Pearl whipped out *the bottle* of champagne. Jayne had a hell of a time stopping her Grammy from opening it, considering she had purchased the $3 bottle of Champale when Jayne was still in elementary school. There was no way on God's green earth that she would even partake of that sour bottle of pink vinegar. Instead, Jayne had shown up with an unopened bottle of Dom Perignon. Knowing the frugality of her Grammy, she also brought along a $13 bottle of Freixenet as her back up. Much as she had suspected, Grammy opted for the Freixenet. The bottle of Dom was still in the back of her fridge.

Soon, she promised herself, there would be something to celebrate and someone special to celebrate with. She just had to be patient. Grammy had taught her years ago not to ask God for something and then sit around like a fool worrying about it. "Let go and let God," Grandma Pearl always said, and she learned.

In high school, when the captain of the math club wanted to go all the way and she was not ready, she heeded her Grammy's words and let Ralph go. The adage still buzzed in her head in college, when the chair of the art department said he would give her a "D" in the class if she would not stay for some extracurricular activities. His activities included helping him relieve the tension in his pants. Jayne took it to God in prayer and left it there. After her professor awarded her the "D" for the course, Jayne took her cell phone and classwork to the Dean and played back the professor's request. At the end of the conference between the three of them, the Dean and her professor, both agreed she deserved that "A".

She loved her Grammy and her wisdom, but Jayne firmly believed that the good Lord helps those who help themselves. Currently, her vision in self-help included a comic book with a kick ass female superhero and matching costume that would be available in local retail stores. Outside of Bling and Storm, there were very few black female heroines in comic books and she wanted to change that. Change would come after she figured out how to make it all happen. She had the talent, but the confidence to do it was another hairy animal.

In the office, she arrived right on time to her desk, with coffee in hand and still a song in her heart. Today, she was leaving for Columbia, South Carolina to attend an anime conference called Banzaicon. This would be her first conference, or con for short, where she would dress in costume for role play. Jayne had two costumes in her car; one for tonight's ball and one for judging. The one for judging she had made herself and was rather proud of it. Nothing could ruin her morning.

Or at least, so she thought. The second hairy animal she had to contend with weekly, was her pod mate and fellow project leader, Frankie Vale, who was a very flatulent man. It did not matter what he ate, or how much or how little he put away. The man was a walking gas giant of methane. It was not just any gas, but the kind of farts that made your eyes water. One day it was so horrendous, she could have sworn his last rip of odiferous death had removed her eyebrows. It made their work relationship contentious. At one point, Jayne had created an online comic strip of Franc the Farter, who was a crime fighter that used noxious fumes to eradicate his enemy. The strip had become very popular, but Jayne forgot to use a pseudonym. Frankie threatened to sue her if she did not take it down. She threatened to sue him for attempted murder with his fumes. He stopped talking to her, relegating their communications to necessity only.

It did not matter much anymore. She brought a face mask for when they had to work together and often after lunch. She opted to work in the conference room when it was not in use. It was easier for them both and definitely easier on her nose.

She kept her eye on the clock as she closed out her daily work At 11:58. She yelled into the bullpen, "Have a great weekend!" Jayne had sent in her monies for the cost of admission into the con. It was time to play dress up and Jayne was ready to make her mark.

- CHAPTER 2-

"Professor!" she exclaimed. She stuck her arm high in the air, as if her fingers could touch the ceiling. When she received no response, she called him again stretching her arm even higher, "Professor! Professor!" She was reacting as a small child in need of a bathroom break, wiggling in the seat. Slowly he looked up. First at the clock, then at Mary Elizabeth, whom he privately named *The Riddler*. As he made his way toward her work station, thoughts of freedom floated through his mind. Only three hours left in the work day.

"Yes, Ms. Jones? How goes your project?" He looked over her shoulder at the computer monitor, visually perplexed at what he was seeing. Today's assignment was to draw the *Popliteal Fossa* to include the nerves, but what he saw on screen closely resembled a diagram on how to steal cable. Stern, firm, and with some tempered resolution, he finally responded, "No, Ms. Jones. You are somewhat off in your drawing. Please consult my instructions and begin again." Mary Elizabeth opened her mouth to protest, but the look he gave her provided caution and did not elicit the reaction she wanted. She too was aware that the professor wanted no part of her shenanigans.

Dr. Toshi Yamaguchi was one, if not the third best, medical illustrator in the country. In his fifth year as Associate Professor at Georgia Regents University in Augusta, he remained firm and detached, but highly proficient in teaching, writing, and publishing. He was on the fast track to tenure. As a Yale graduate, he had many choices of what he wanted to do and where he wanted to teach. At the age of 30, his real dream was comics. In an ideal world, he would be on staff at Marvel as the lead artist for his own original designs and characters.

In this world, he had broken his wrist in a motorcycle accident, causing some damage to the nerves in his right hand. His parents were broken hearted that he would never be able to hold a scalpel, which was fine by him, but it also limited his ability to hold charcoals, paint brushes, and colored pencils. It wasn't really such a disappointment to Toshi, since he had not truly wanted to be a doctor. In all honesty, he didn't desire to be an academic either. Even though he had the letters, people called him doctor, and his parents were appeased. Somewhat. They now craved grandchildren.

It wasn't about to happen. He liked being single. He loved the freedom to move about and spend his money as he saw fit. The small student loans he had taken out for his education were paid off. The down payment for his house was still in a bank account drawing interest and there was no one to nag him about where he was going this weekend, or why he was spending so much money on frivolous items so he could play dress up.

To Toshi Yamaguchi, fandom was about more than dressing up as your favorite hero. Fandom was a way of life, but also an expensive hobby. His girlfriend Ai, often complains when he departs for conferences for several days, stating that he is going to go broke frolicking with his friends. Often he would joke with her about fandom, coming back with a quick retort, "it costs to play with the big boys."

Ai reminds him weekly that it costs to play with a grown woman as well. In his mind, Ai was an unwanted expense and a distraction. The sex was mediocre, leaving her place in his space, dwindling in value. Toshi checked the clock again. It was almost time. "Do not forget your homework assignments which are due on Tuesday. Remember the upper and lower lateral and medial borders of the *Popliteal Fossa* are due in eAssignment and hard copy in color when you walk in the door."

Mary Elizabeth's hand flew up again, but Toshi ignored her. Many of his student surveys would come back, with comments that he appeared to be unfeeling. That was untrue. He felt everything. Right now, the main emotion coursing through his body was disdain. Mary Elizabeth had a crush on him and used any means she could find to get his attention. He'd had it and he wanted her out the door. It was time for the weekend and he had a conference to get to as well as a Samurai suit to get packed. "Have a great weekend," he told the students as they walked out the door. He looked at Mary Elizabeth, "If you are thinking about how to complete the assignment, then you are thinking too much. Draw, draw, and draw some more." A quick closing of his MacBook and he was out the door. He popped his head into his office and waved goodbye to the office assistant, Ms. Banks, before heading to the parking garage.

Before he reached the car, he received a call from Ai. "Toshi, we need to talk." Again, another distraction. He responded in a quick clipped tone, "Fine. Meet me at 5 at the Soy Noodle House on Broad Street." He did not give her a chance to respond. He hung up and hurried home. Everything was ready to go, he just needed to load the car.

He was on his way to Columbia, South Carolina for Banzaicon. This was the first con where he was entering the costume competition. The larger cons are intimidating to some people and even more so to Toshi as an academic, but at this con he was ready to take on the challenge. He had never been to a smaller conference and was excited to debut his new Silver Samurai costume.

In his heart, at each conference he attended, he hoped to find a friend, or someone who understood him. Someone who would appreciate the craftsmanship of his homemade suit. He knew that Ai, was never going to be that person.

Toshi arrived at the Soy Noodle House at 4:50 and picked a table in the corner close to the window, but also close to the front door. In his mind, this conversation was going to be short. Ai arrived five minutes later, still wearing her work clothing and lab coat. At five foot seven with shiny black hair, a perfect set of teeth and a warm smile, Toshi was filled with regret that he could not find it in himself to love her the way she deserved to be loved. Ai Tomita was a great dentist who was loved by all of her patients, anyone who came into contact with her, and others who thrived just being in her light. Yet for Toshi, he felt dim whenever he was with her; further playing into the irony of their relationship. It was more troubling to him that her name meant "love". For him, he could only get as far as a cordial fondness for her. She whined incessantly about him being cold and unfeeling, but he did not know how to express to her that he had strong feelings about almost everything else. As she walked up to the door, his

Olivia Gaines

heart should have skipped a beat to see her approaching, instead what he felt bordered on apathy.

He rose to greet Ai, helping her with her chair, before reseating himself. He had already ordered a pot of hot tea. She poured him a fresh cup and one for herself. There it was, that condescending sigh. It was a sound that curled his toes inside his shoes. A sound of disappointment and angst in one exhalation, followed by a cluck of her tongue and a nibble on her bottom lip. Then came the condescending words that grabbed a man by his balls and shook him to his core. The private nickname he had given her was *Ball Buster*. "Toshi, I was hoping that this weekend you would change your mind about the *play thing* in Columbia and go with me to Atlanta, to be with our friends."

Ai's condescending attitude had rubbed him the wrong way, especially the way she said *play thing*. He wondered how much it would hurt her feelings if she knew he felt pretty much the same about her role in his life. At this point in this relationship, Toshi had already resigned himself to be free, which made him fail to filter his words. "I was hoping you would change your mind and come with me."

Ai sipped at her tea, "I am sorry, but I must say this. You are going to have to decide Toshi. Either we will have a life together, or you can continue to play your dress up superhero games."

"Fine," he said, as he returned his teacup to its saucer and rose to leave.

She was shocked. "So does this mean you are coming to Atlanta with me?" He rested his hand upon her shoulder, giving her a saddened look.

"No, it means that I am headed to Columbia to do my *play thing*."

Ai's mouth was moving but no words were coming out. Toshi leaned forward, taking her chin in his hand, while pushing the flailing jaws together. "Let me help you Ai. It means that I am not choosing you."

She stared at him with lips now taut. He made an attempt to soften the blow. "I like you enough to let you go so that you can be with someone else, who can be all the things you want and need in a husband." He lowered his head and placed a light kiss upon her cheek. He was going to be late to the ball if he didn't get a move on.

Before Ai could say anything to him, he stood in front of the window and took out his cell phone. She watched his practiced fingers move across the screen, and knew he had turned it off for the weekend. It was one of the many traits that bugged her to no end about Toshi, but indecisiveness was not one of them. Once he made up his mind that was the end.

Toshi Yamaguchi had just dumped her. When he had to make the choice between dressing up as a crime fighting superhero and drawing comics, or being with her, he opted to be the superhero. In her mind, his actions were villainous. He had just made a down payment on a new enemy and she was not going to let this go lightly. There would be no way to explain to her parents how she had managed to run off another potential husband.

CHAPTER 3

At 4:00 pm on Friday afternoon, Toshi dressed as Gambit from the X-Men and headed downstairs to the hotel lobby to mix and mingle with the other conference attendees. Many con junkies came early to meet the prettiest ladies and maybe score a conference hook up. This had only happened twice for him, but he was single again, so his mind was open to the possibilities. Slipping into the black seamless pants, and picking up a deck of cards, he would hold up an ace of spades to any woman who caught his eye. Thus far, there had been only two. So many of these attendees were very young and if any reminded him of a student, he shied away.

Vendors had set up earlier in the afternoon. At such a small con, there aren't many writers, artists, or designers present, but Toshi had been tapped to teach two of the classes on Saturday. One in the morning and the other in the afternoon. He was looking forward to it. As he passed by the vendor room, he nearly kept walking but was halted by a vision of delightfulness bent over into a bin of buttons and tchotchkes. In his mind, he hoped it was a woman. The purple Lycra pants, black hair, and a glimpse of side boob said female. It would be most uncomfortable for him if she were not. Feeling confident, he leaned down and whispered close to her ear, "that has to be the most perfect ass I have ever seen."

The princess with the perfect posterior turned slowly, raised her body to full height, and faced Toshi with a look of disgust, "you do realize you said that out loud, right?"

The directness of her tone made Toshi step back. He

was also surprised to see that she was a black woman, with a whole lot of attitude. The heels she wore gave her an additional few inches in height, but he imagined her in stocking feet to stand only at five feet maybe four inches. She had full lips and deep, wide set brown eyes that looked like pools of liquid milk chocolate. She had a gap in her teeth and the cutest nose he had ever seen on any woman. Initially, he had thought the hair to be a wig, but as he stared at her, it did not take long to understand it was actually her hair.

"I meant to say it loud enough for you to hear me," he added with a cockiness that was unlike him. Being dressed as Gambit, he felt stronger, more powerful, and far more daring than he should. "At least I didn't ask you to sit it in my lap." He stood with his legs shoulder width apart, his arms folded across his midriff, calling her out. By making such a bold move, Toshi also noticed that his heart rate had increased.

Toshi thought she looked extremely hot dressed as Bling, and much like the comic book character, attitude and angst radiated from her. Jayne was staring at the costumed man, but it was unclear if behind the mask he was Japanese or Chinese. What was evident was the man was arrogant and thought she was an easy mark. She moved closer to him, bringing a smaller smile to his face as she extended her index finger, wiggling it, beckoning him to come closer. "I like the costume Gambit and I like how you decided to take a gamble, but I have to let you know something very important." She paused to drive home the words she was going to hit him with, "but...."

Toshi leaned closer to hear what she had to say. He

placed his hand upon his chest in mock chivalry, but it was really an effort to quell the rapid beating of his heart. She smiled as she delivered the words, "you are an asshole."

He reacted as if he had been slapped. She pushed him to the side and walked passed him heading into the conference registration area. He watched her sashay away with more than a casual interest. The initial assessment had not changed. That was still the most perfect ass he had ever seen in his life, but the woman who owned it, was a handful. He found himself with a very wide grin that harbored a very playful thought. *That ass was a perfect handful as well.*

Toshi felt stimulated by her. Her words had hurt his feelings. That was something that had never happened before and he did not like the idea of her thinking of him as an asshole. He called after her. "There you go again, just walking away from the team."

The lady stopped dead in her tracks. Giving just enough of a turn. "I was never truly a part of the team."

She walked away. The faint scent of her perfume still lingered in the air. It was mixed with whatever she used on her hair. Toshi's body reacted. Emotions flooded through him and confusion was knocking at the chunks of blockades that had grown into his cerebral cortex. He had slept with a black woman before, actually, all races of women, but never really considered it anything other than a physical release. Yet that creamy skinned vixen, moved him. For the first time in several years, he felt something stirring him up.

This was going to be a great weekend.

Jayne was an artist and a very good one, but there were two things Jayne was not; easy and easy going. Comic books and painting were her first love, cosplaying was her second, with costume designing coming in a close third. Men were something she had little time for, although her body frequently reminded her of the important role they played in the life of a woman. More so if she planned to procreate. However, children were nowhere on her list of things to get done in her lifetime. Her experience with men had been limited, with only one serious sexual partner to her credit, whom she seldom spoke of nor had many fond memories. Alex had been the first man she been intimate with. Time was moving along at such a clip, that there was little time left to worry about the insignificance of a warm body next to her in bed. Although most conferences served as hookups for the lonely and disenfranchised, for her, this conference was her opportunity to display her newest anime outfit, make a few contacts, and hopefully have a remote chance of winning a prize.

The insulting man in the vendor shop had been just another testosterone filled moron who wanted to get into her pants before getting into her head. Her eyes grew wide at the mere thought of the stories she could tell about the misunderstandings from men who wanted to be a part of her world, but really did not understand what she was trying to accomplish. Jayne wanted to be a costume designer and design an original comic book character.

She lived art. She drank art. In her free time, she breathed comics and she knew this year was going to be her swan song. This year she was going to debut her comic book even if she had to self-publish it on Kindle or Blurb. The work was good. The script was even better. The art work was high caliber, but it was lacking something. She could not put her finger on it, but there was still some time to figure out the defunct.

At 28 years old, Jayne had scored her job with Cawley Public Relations after an internship her senior year in art school. She had not planned to stay with the company for five years, but it was a good fit. Moving back home had not been an easy decision, but her Grammy was getting up in age and the break up with Alex had nearly cost her the small amount of sanity that was left over after sketching and scribbling fictional characters. Occasionally, she would make it to a con and get to dress up as one of her favorite characters as well.

Cosplaying to her was a step beyond *LARPing* and far more fun. Cosplay was a great way for costume designers to get together and show off their craft. The conferences allowed other comic book, fantasy, and science fiction lovers to get together and play games. To her, there was a big difference between cosplaying and LARPing. LARPing is live action role-playing, where the characters actually create scenarios and reenact scenes. That was just a bit too geeky for Jayne's taste. However, getting a chance to don a costume and become the character, changed the way she felt about herself. She loved how the costumes made her feel. In costume, she was powerful and pretty.

Commanding. Admired. Loved.

None of the things she exhibited in real life. In real life, she was a petite weird black woman, with crazy hair, a gap in her teeth and dreams that men did not understand. Even her mother didn't understand her. She felt at times that her friends were humoring her when they listened to her stories. Eventually, she had stopped sharing her ideas. None of what she said was coming to fruition, so it was all just a pipe dream. Or so it had been. This weekend, she was going to change her fate. Winning this costume contest was going to change her storyline. This was going to move her dream forward.

Something made her come to a stop. Besides the several people wanting to take photos with her, she felt eyes boring into her back. Slowly she turned around and spotted the Gambit dude still watching her. Camera flashes were going off as she posed with a few children, two men, and the last one she took, she posed in a fighting stance. The shock she felt when she realized she was posing with Gambit was almost too much. The charge between the two of them was palpable.

A small crowd began to gather as Gambit slid into another pose. Not to be outdone, she altered her stance to a second pose matching him. The crowd began to chant as Gambit pulled playing cards from his pockets and sent them flying into the crowd. In a flash, he grabbed her by the hand and pulled her close, segueing into a third pose that caused the crowd to go mad. He held her close with his hands in the small of her back. She could feel the power of his thighs pressing against her own while the male part of him pressed to her delicate part as he hoisted her thigh to ensure she felt his enthusiasm. The kids were all smiling. The flashes from the cameras had nearly blinded her, but she got a grip on herself. Without making a scene, Jayne pulled away, bowed to the audience, and kowtowed to Gambit, making eye contact with him while mouthing the words, "asshole."

She rounded the corner with Toshi on her heels, but the throng of people closed in on him wanting more pictures. He would not be able to get to her in time and he felt antsy, charged up, excited and ready for.......whatever. He wasn't sure. Toshi knew that whatever it was, it included that woman.

Jayne rounded the corner, out of breath and full of conflicted emotions. When Gambit took her hand, the sparks that flew up her arm were electric. The man was a pig to even pull her in close like that, so she could feel the pure maleness of his body. It was offensive! Yet, she had never experienced such an intense feeling with anyone.

Chapter 4-

The light from the ceiling was cascading down on the dais, illuminating the strong facial features of the instructor. Jayne watched with some amusement as she eyed his strong jawline, high cheek bones, and Asian eyes. His irises were dark, giving him an aura of mystery, intrigue, and a hint of something she could not mash her finger into. Something felt familiar about him, but his skill set with shadowing was amazing. Each stroke of his wrist sparked her imagination as he tinted the panels of each comic book cell, demonstrating how to darken areas of the body to simulate motion. It was uncertain if the attraction she was feeling derived from his talent or the confidence which radiated from his role as an instructor. Either way, Dr. Toshi Yamaguchi was sexy as hell to her.

She had never dated an Asian man, nor had any interest in doing so until now, but this man was giving her second thoughts. First that Gambit dude, now him. She thought back to her philosophy professor, who found Freudian meaning in every occurrence. She had met two very different Asian men in two days. One she found completely repulsive. The other, she found fascinating. The soft, confident way in which he delivered the two hour block of instruction was followed along with a trancelike state of conference goers. Jayne found herself hypnotized by his words and enlightened with his instruction.

Banzaicon was only the fourth conference that Jayne had attended in her life. Outside of her run-in with that Gambit guy, she was enjoying herself immensely. After the check in on Friday night, she noticed two new classes had been added to the schedule. *Shadowing Techniques for Comics*, and *Creating Original Characters*. She jumped at the chance to take the courses. Thus far she had not been disappointed. The instructor was absolutely phenomenal as he used his tablet to sketch out designs, while having the audience follow along. Jayne was even more impressed that he left the make shift stage to walk through the room to check the progress of each of the attendee's work before he moved on to the next technique. At some instance during the instruction, it was twice as impressive that Dr. Yamaguchi laid eyes on every single drawing in the room, providing quasi one on one with every attendee in the session. This was doubly impressive, considering it was standing room only. The younger fans were eating it up, when he looked at their pages, giving canned responses of "good, a little darker here," or "great job." Jayne even found she puffed up a bit when he glanced at her work, stating "good eye for detail." Now she felt foolish because he smelled good too. She was fighting back the urge to get all goofy like many of the women on the front row were.

In the final steps of the drawing, Dr. Yamaguchi employed an old technique of using time lapse to dictate shadow. "Start your shadowing technique at noon. To simulate running, shift the shadow to two o'clock, then three in the next frame." Jayne had never considered such a thing, but when he demonstrated his idea in three panels, the whole room said, "ahhh." Before long, the two hours were up. Dr. Yamaguchi thanked everyone for coming.

The young women flocked to the instructor as Jayne sat, still sketching out an idea that had come to mind based on his last words. No other course had been planned in this room until after lunch, so she continued to work, drafting through her ideas. She was listening, but not listening. As the instructor escorted the women to the door, his deep voice reminded her of the bad guy in the Karate movies who always came into the whore house and drank up all the Sake. He told the young ladies, "I must leave now to grab a bite to eat, before the next session. Excuse me." She found herself smiling as she mimicked, "ah, yes, Mr. Woo, so glad to have you in our fine establishment." She let out a pretend courtesan giggle like she had heard the Asian women do in the movies.

One of the young ladies asked him to join her, but he declined, saying he had already committed to having lunch with a friend. Jayne heard that part from his practiced lines and just imagined his new friend as some dim-witted ingénue in a Sailor Moon costume. Dr. Yamaguchi's deep voice was rich with southern undertones and dripping with the practiced ease of a very expensive education. The ladies sounded disappointed, but he turned to Jayne asking, "Are we ready my friend? I am starving."

Jayne looked over her shoulder to see who he was talking to and spying no one else in the room, she quickly realized it was her. The look on his face was asking for a rescue, which made her gather her things and say, "sure thing ole pal. Ready when you are."

He opened the outer door for her and led the way to the hotel restaurant. "I only have an hour or so before the next session, so I hope you don't mind eating here and..." he paused, cutting her a side glance. "... You do know I heard you back there?"

She gulped, lowering her head in shame at the racial

stereotype she had projected, mumbling an apology. She would make it up to him over lunch. Jayne had not realized how hungry she had been until she smelled the food. The hotel restaurant did not seem like a good idea, but most of the conference attendees were headed out for pizza or sandwiches, which left the lobby seating open. Toshi pulled out a chair for her then went to the bar to grab a couple of menus.

What are you doing here with him? Wild thoughts ran through her mind that it was going to be the prickliest lunch ever, but to her surprise it was not. The conversation was light after he thanked her for coming to his rescue. His voice remained steady as he said, "I love to attend cons, but I am uncertain if many of the attendees are even old enough to drink, so I err on the side of caution."

"You seem to have a great number of groupies for an artist."

He smiled as he raised his hand for the waiter to come over. "Art is sexy. I am an artist." He arched an eyebrow indicating that she needed to deduct the final formula.

"You are a sexy artist," she said in a flat voice. It was more of a question than a logical deduction.

"Really, you think so? I thank you." He let out a chuckle before adding, "have you decided what you would like?"

Jayne looked at the menu and decided on a Chicken Caesar Salad, as she watched him over the rim of her glasses. He ordered a pot of tea. Since she had been insulting before, she felt she needed him to understand that she was not ignorant of his culture. When the tea arrived, she stood and kowtowed to him while filling his tea cup. She poured a bit for herself, then took a seat. He watched her with some interest, but his facial expressions were indecipherable.

As the food arrived, he ate rice with chopped vegetables and Sautéed Chicken, as he reviewed notes and sketches. It felt peculiar to sit here like this with him, sharing a meal, yet it was perfectly comfortable. They were sharing a space, but not sharing each other. He had not asked her name and she had not volunteered to provide him with it.

She looked up from her salad and found him staring at her. "What?" she asked.

"There is something about you that speaks to me," he said as he cut into the last chunk of chicken.

Jayne wasn't sure if it was a pick up line or another smart ass comment. "Thank you," was all she could muster. He sat there waiting for her to say something.

"What?"

"I don't know," he said as he shrugged his shoulders. "There is something about you. Your qi is calling to me." His heart rate had picked up again. This was an uncommon reaction for him around a woman. Although he had been with a few black women before, she *felt* different. It unsettled him.

"I thought Chi was a Chinese term," she said while continuing to eat her meal but looked at her watch.

"Qi, or, chi and even Xi, are terms that are in several languages. All meaning life force. I don't know what it is about you...." His words trailed off as he eyed the check.

There was a quick demonstration on Kimono making in one of the break out rooms that she wanted to see before going to his next session on creating original characters. She picked up her purse, grabbed a twenty from her wallet, and laid it on the table. "Well, today is not the day for you to figure it out." She bowed again and told him to take care as she headed down the hall to the demonstration.

There was something about him as well that made her feel off kilter. She didn't like it... not one bit. Playing with a man like that always came at a price and she was unwilling to pay the toll.

The afternoon class was equally phenomenal as Dr. Yamaguchi showed the attendees how to use a favorite personal photo as a template to create an original character. The sound of pencils against sketch pads making strokes and shading, radiated throughout the crowded room. As he had earlier in the morning, Toshi milled through the throng of sketchers, who had laid out on the floor, leaned against the walls, and occupied every chair, as they presented their work to him at the midway point. The latter portion of the session, he taught his makeshift students the importance of drawing muscles, muscle tone, and muscle sinew. Jayne was amazed at how much better her earlier sketch looked after applying these newly learned techniques. She found herself staring at him absently.

As if he felt her eyes upon him, Toshi turned, catching her unaware, meeting her gaze. His heartbeat sped up when their eyes connected. *What was it about this woman?* He quickly shifted his focus so his body would not betray him. At the end of the session, he was flocked by conference goers with a ton of questions. He looked for her, but she had disappeared.

Jayne was uncomfortable with the intensity of the

connection she was feeling with the good doctor. Maybe she was responding to his artistic ability. It was a foolhardy assessment. The woman in her was responding to the man in him. She shook it off and headed to her room to change for the Cosplay event at 6 pm.

Jayne was planning to debut her costume as Pirotess, from *Record of Lodoss War*. Uncertainty was ringing through her mind as she wondered if anyone would know who she was or even *get* the character. It was all she had, so she was going to go with it. Earlier, she felt a great deal of confidence. Now she was uncertain. Three weeks had been spent creating the costume, ensuring that every minute detail had been covered, even working her body out extra hard. Threads, stitches, and fabric choice were all very important when designing a costume. Even more important was the flow of material when on the body. It was these details that she hoped would give her a placing in the show. She checked her hair, her makeup, and adjusted the girls in the suit.

The time had flown by and it was time to head downstairs.

Entering the elevator, there were several Lolita's, *Dragon Ball Z* characters along with other sub characters from *Sailor Moon*. The show stopper was the *Silver Samurai* in the lobby. The detail of the costume was bordering on amazing as many walked up to him to touch the leather and fabricated pieces. As Jayne walked by him, he drew his sword, placing it in front of her to block her path. She could not see his face, but immediately knew it was the jerk from last night who was dressed as Gambit. A quick shove with her hand and she pushed the sword aside and made her way to the judging stage. The costumes had been judged earlier yesterday, so tonight was just a formality.

One by one the characters filed on stage, role-playing in the costumes and showing off their handy work. The Silver Samurai was a skilled martial artist and swordsman. The audience oohed and ahhed as he maneuvered from posing to performing high flying kicks for two and a half minutes. Jayne felt sexy as Pirotess when she climbed on stage. She posed and showed a bit of skin as she sauntered across the platform.

The waiting was brief since many of the costumes had already been judged. Three of the *Dragon Ball Z* characters had placed with honorable mentions. An online comic series had received third place for one of the characters, which received a great audience response. Jayne was excited when she was awarded second place. The Silver Samurai received first place. Standing close to him, she understood why. He looked really good in the costume with his muscles bulging through the taut leather, his shiny black hair hanging from under the helmet, and those intense eyes gazing through the eye slots.

The winners were all lined up on stage for a quick photo op and then the group began to disperse. The samurai touched her arm beckoning her to follow him. She trailed him into a corner and he removed his helmet. Jayne's eyes were wide when she realized Gambit, the Silver Samurai, and Dr. Toshi Yamaguchi was the same person!

Toshi asked her, "What are your plans for tonight?"

"I plan to go to the party and have a drink or two," she told him waiting to see if he would ask her to dinner.

"I am heading to my room." He turned and began to

walk away. "Come with me." It was said with such matter-of-factness that Jayne stood there blinking after him. He looked back to see why she was not walking along with him. He extended to her his hand in a quieter request.

"What am I going to do in your room?"

Toshi's eyebrows went up, "I was hoping... me."

She couldn't believe it. "You know you said that out loud?"

Toshi moved closer to her. "Would it have more impact if I whispered it instead?"

Jayne was disgusted with him. All of her admiration for his talent had flown out the window. She tried to step around him, but he extended his hand to stop her. "There is something about you that stirs my blood. I want to be with you. I am being honest by telling you what I want."

"It seems like you would want to know my name first, Professor. And you know what...?" she paused with her hand on her hip. "I was wrong about you. You are not an asshole, you are a *fucking* asshole."

Toshi moved so quickly Jayne was startled. He stood toe to toe with her. His breath, caressing her cheek as he leaned into her ear. "Pirotess, Bling, or whatever you want to be called, you are amazing. You are a talented artist and you are making me crazy, but I understand. There have been so many men that have lied to you. The truth is hard for you to accept."

"I can accept the truth just fine. I don't accept you wanting to use me as a personal plaything."

He lowered his voice to a whisper, using a sensual and sultry tone. "I don't plan to use you. I plan to give you hours of pleasure." He said it in such a way, that her body said yes, but her mouth said, "thanks, but no."

She stepped around him and headed for the elevator. The idea of going to the party no longer seemed fun. In the morning she would check out and head home. That jerk off had just ruined her night. She hoped he spent the rest of the night doing just that as well.

Unfortunately, her wish for him would probably not come true. A flock of women surrounded him. Some were subtle, while others were direct, using their bodies to gain his attention. She looked back at him once more and was surprised to see his attention was not on the women, but instead on her. Jayne's brain was screaming at her to keep moving, but her body was crying, begging her to go back. She shook her head at him, then moved on to the elevator.

Friends with Benefits

Olivia Gaines

Chapter One

The view from the balcony was often an inviting scene. Below, lounging about the pool, were beautiful people who wanted to be seen or were waiting patiently to be picked up and made relevant. The climb to importance in standing and social status which would be determined by the longevity of the next person they chose as a bed partner. If chosen correctly, a book deal or a reality show could be possible, but it took time. It took money. It took the right clothing, but more importantly, it took being seen with the right person.

For him, the beautiful people were as misleading as the pool itself; crystalline and inviting, but filled with bacteria. Caution was not germane to the chemicals and salts that the staff added to keep down the algae and fungi, because at the end of the day, someone always pees in the pool. In the middle of the night moans and grunts could be heard by people who think it is a good idea to copulate in water. He never swam in the pool, nor ventured to lounge at its side. The whole area was shark-infested and at times, he felt like a defenseless guppy.

Modern relationships had become confusing and left him wanting. What he yearned for and wanted was unclear, but it was very clear that he no longer wanted what he was receiving. As he stood on the balcony, he noticed the ample-chested young beauty eyeing him. He raised his beer bottle to acknowledge that she had been seen. She raised her bikini top to extend an invitation for him to come downstairs to see more. A nod of his head was given to the young ingénue, before he retreated into his condo, closed the blinds and turned on the game. That was some nonsense he wanted no part of; been there, did her.

It had crossed his mind on several occasions to put the condo up for sale and purchase a three- or four-bedroom home in Marietta or Kennesaw to get out of the city. He definitely needed to get out of this building, since he had slept with almost every single female tenant. Married women often invited him for coffee, pie or some other obscure reason to enter their front door, so in the middle of the night or the afternoon, he could slip out the back. As much as it pained him to say, he was tired of sex.

Copulation had begun to feel like a chore more than a want or a need. Today was one of those days when he neither needed nor wanted any. A private challenge was issued to himself; it was time to find out how long he could actually go without sex. The laptop sat on the table and a quick flip of the top, opened an application and printed out this and next month's calendar. It had already been a week, so he crossed those days off on the calendar and took them to the kitchen to pin them on the fridge. This could be done; he needed to know what he was made of and how much sex actually influenced his decision-making ability.

Grayson Broche took pride in his appearance although his hair was never quite combed. He always felt that his slightly disheveled locks added to his tall, swarthy appeal, adding an air of mystery to him. Few people could even fathom that he was an entertainment lawyer who represented some of the biggest acts in the movie and the music industry. Others could not understand how he lived in Atlanta and represented those who worked in

Hollywood. It was simple, word of mouth. He was good. His team was better. He was an attorney who was honest.

The days of hands-on with the talent were behind him and he only dealt with producers, management and the upper echelons of the business. Young actors and talent still trying to find themselves were old hat and old news. The phone calls in the middle of the night from starlets who were drinking and driving, incarcerated or plain inebriated, no longer had his number. It seemed so difficult for them to understand, as an entertainment lawyer, he negotiated their contracts and took a percentage. He was not their parent and he was not interested in babysitting their neurosis. Eleven years in the business of entertainment law had taught him one cardinal rule: never sleep with the help.

As a young man, fresh out of law school, many thought he was nuts to open his own firm without any seasoning. Who needed seasoning when you already knew the flavoring? Many young artists were being ripped off and cheated by unscrupulous business practices and companies who took advantage of their naiveté. Broche & Associates specialized in artists across all genres including stage, television, music, film, and even production. Grayson's reputation was sound, his practices, fair and his team was completely above par. It was instilled in every person who worked with and for him: hands off the talent. Friends, groupies and tagalongs were okay, but the clientele was a no-no. Sex complicated matters. When matters become complicated, so does the money. He made it abundantly clear to the team—don't screw with my money.

Overall, Grayson considered himself to be a good guy

with a few bad habits. His main fault was he had poor taste in women. At 36 years old, he was ready for something different, but he had to have some clarity on where he was going. His best friend Charlize often told him he thinks with his eyes. Grayson had no idea what that meant, but she was the only constant in his life. They had a ten-year friendship built on trust, understanding, and no hanky-panky. Charlize was Grayson's rock and his best friend.

And that is what prompted Grayson Broche to start thinking a bit differently.

Chapter Two

Charlize climbed onto the flexion distraction table to begin the realignment of the quarterback's right hip. She was amazed at how whiny he was during treatment and how tough he seemed on the field in last week's Falcon's game. After positioning herself under his thigh, she hooked her arm under his shoulder and counted to three. One push, a shove and a twist, she heard the familiar pop while watching relief wash over Mr. Crybaby's face.

For the past five years she had served as one of the sports medicine doctors for the Atlanta Falcons. Doc Feelme was the nickname the players gave her, but Dr. Charlize Filleman is the best in the field. It was a bidding war for her talent between the Braves, the Hawks, the Thrashers and the Falcons to get her on staff. What made her a hot commodity was she was a certified chiropractor as well as a licensed M.D. She worked on the best bodies in the business and was surrounded by rich men with too much money and gigantic egos. Women were always flocking around the training camps trying to be seen, or wanting to be a trophy. It all disgusted her.

On occasions, during the off season, Charlize prided herself on getting away for a fabulous vacation, then back to work. The thought had crossed her mind to open her own practice and patent some of her training techniques, but last year, her best friend Grayson had convinced her to write a cookbook for the pro athlete. With his connections, he scored her a sweet book deal and personally represented her in the negotiations. He was a great friend and the type of guy who had principles. He taught her early on when

she took the job with the team, don't sleep with the help—
it diminishes your authority.

It was great advice. The players often asked her out or
bought her expensive gifts that she refused. She watched
several of the physical therapists on her staff get entangled
with the athletes only to be humiliated in the end when the
player married some real housewife of Atlanta type. New
staff members were warned in orientation, "I am the
standard, do as I do, and you will have a long career.
Please, be smart, don't sleep with the players. If you
fraternize, you are fired. I will not bother to hear your side
of the story, you are gone."

Why she bothered was beyond her; every season, there
was always one. It took her two seasons to get smart and
only hired women who were not into men, or women who
were a couple of steps below attractive. It was unfair, but
it cut down on fraternization and stabilized her staff. The
past three years, the team came back to camp with the
same therapist which made all involved happy; without a
learning curve, worked moved at the right pace.

Charlize just wished she was happy as well and could
find someone who could also move at her speed. She had
not dated in three years and was completely bored with the
dating process. It befuddled her to no end why men
believed that dinner and a movie equated to coming to her
home and bouncing up and down on her all night. It was
not her style. A connection had to be present. There had
to be respect, understanding, and a spark. Heck, she would
be happy to have dinner and conversation about something
other than football. She worked with the team. She didn't
play *on* the team. *No*, I cannot get you an autograph. *No*, I
will not tell you a player's physical condition so you can bet

on the game. And I will definitely, never, sneak you a picture of a player during the rehabilitation process.

The only male company she kept in the past three years was her weekly dinners with Grayson. The conversations were lively, the access he had to shows were phenomenal and she truly felt his friendship was one of the more precious things in her life. She never wanted it to be complicated or convoluted. She was honest with him when she did not understand some of his choices in women, but never questioned, just supported, and was there to pick up the pieces when it inevitably went awry. This year, she was planning a nice getaway to Kauai, and had considered asking him to come along; she just wasn't sure how he would take it. Also under consideration, during the holidays, his family always had big lavish spreads, and she was uncertain if he wanted to forgo the annual tradition for some exotic sun. She smiled when she thought of him; a bright spot in her life.

He must have been thinking about her as well, her cell phone chimed and she answered on the second ring, "Howdy, Partner!"

"You free for dinner tonight?"

"Sure, my place or yours?"

"You come to me, and bring some wine, all I have is beer."

Charlize knew the tone in his voice, something was on his mind. She shut everything down in the office and headed home first for a change of clothing. When he asked for the bottle of wine, she knew they would empty it and she would be staying over in the guest room. Whatever was on his mind must be a dilemma that was heavily weighted,

Olivia Gaines

she just hoped it wasn't another love interest gone wrong.

Chapter Three

Grayson's condo was located in midtown Atlanta in the heart of the mass of traffic, college students, and aspiring artists. His office was not far away from his home and Grayson often rode his motorcycle into work. Most of his clientele thought he was attempting to portray the proverbial bad boy with the Valkyrie, and was almost disappointed when they found out that he rode it mainly to save on gas. Charlize often laughed because her friend was such a dude.

During her first visit to his condo, she was not surprised to find the black leather couch, glass end tables, and statues of a large bathing Hebe. The painting over the couch was homage to the 80's and the bedroom was reminiscent of a broke pimp's younger days. It was the leather padded headboard decorated with purple studs which made her laugh out loud. The only thing worse were the bedside lamps which were covered in red velvet and the shades were embossed with the words L.O.V.E. and cut out hearts. When the lamps were turned on, they cast L.O.V.E. on the walls. Without even thinking, she unplugged both lamps and took them to the trash; he attempted to argue and she held up her finger for him to be quiet. There could be no logic, reasoning, or rationale for such hideous items. Purse and keys in hand she only said, "car, now...." and drove him to a furniture store. Together, they chose a soft brown suede sofa and matching recliner with a cherry wood coffee table accented with strong, clean lines. As her gift to him, she purchased the matching ottoman and end tables, and bought two new lamps for his bedroom. A gentle nudge was provided and Grayson was convinced that the new headboard was his idea.

While they were out, Charlize pointed out the matching bookcases which would be perfect for his media collection and books. The paintings were replaced by show posters autographed by his clients. The bathing Hebe was replaced by a ficus and some dieffenbachia's, which flourished in the morning sun. The leather couches were moved to the third bedroom which now served as a man cave. The hideous headboard was now in the guest bedroom along with the sexist end tables that said "seduce me." To her surprise, Grayson asked for her assistance in picking out an appropriately sized dining room set to compliment the new living room furniture. It made her heart happy to rid his home of the glass and wrought iron set with the matching fabric covered chairs. His home now looked like a settled and established gentleman lived in it, versus a love shack for the misunderstood.

The kitchen was her favorite. For a condo, it was far roomier and more spacious than expected. Grayson had made great choices on the appliances; they considered themselves foodies who loved to cook and very rarely ate out. One thing the two friends truly shared in common was a love of health and nutrition. Each week, they sought a new recipe to try out and the best selections were chosen and put to the side. After many years, the box of recipes which had been tweaked and adjusted were now sorted and being added to her new cookbook.

Tonight, for dinner they were making roast pork with sage and pecan pesto, green beans with toasted almonds with lemon and dessert was a fruit salad with lemon mint syrup. It became important to Charlize that nothing be wasted, each ingredient should be used completely and the meal should offer more than one serving. Grayson had already prepared the pork loin in the apple cider brine and when she arrived, they chatted while he browned the pork loin in the pan, she trimmed the green beans, minced the garlic and sautéed it in a pan.

It would take the roast an hour to cook and she opened the wine, poured them both a glass before she began to prepare the fruit for dessert. As she placed the items in the fridge, she noticed the calendar, "Are you counting down to something special?"

"Nope, those are the number of days I have not had sex," he said plainly as he wiped down the counters. Charlize dropped the glass bowl and began to check him for fever. "Wait, my medical bag is in the car, let me go and grab it," she told him as he watched her with a facial expression that was less than amused. He added the pecans, sage and other ingredients into the food processor to make the pesto, now he was feeling a little insecure for sharing this with her so soon. It had only been 14 days. This wasn't a big feat for him, but his mind was clearer. He cleaned up the glass from the floor and went over it with a Swiffer to pick up any remaining shards.

Charlize realized he was serious and apologized, "I'm sorry, I thought maybe something was wrong."

"Something is wrong," he said as he pulsed the processor, "it's my personal life; right now, the only good thing in it, is you."

"That's really sweet, but seriously, why are you abstaining?"

"I need to know more about myself. I need some clarity.

I want...."

He got quiet.

She poured more wine and waited. The years of friendship had taught her to wait for him to collect his thoughts. Working with type *A* males had also taught her to be quiet and not fill in the spaces with assumptions and idle chatter. He would tell her when he had gathered the right words.

"I want something very similar to what you and I have, but with benefits." Charlize dropped the wine glass.

And that was how Grayson Broche opened the discussion to starting a relationship that included being more than just friends.

About the Author

Olivia Gaines is the author of numerous bestselling novellas and books, including *Two Nights in Vegas*, *A Few More Nights*, and has had several number one best sellers with *The Blakemore Files* including *Being Mrs. Blakemore* and *Shopping with Mrs. Blakemore*.

She lives in Augusta, GA, with her husband, son and snotty cat, Katness Evermean.

Connect with Olivia on her Facebook page at http://on.fb.me/1eorEAr or her website at http://oliviagaines.com.

Coming Soon

A big box bookstore was coming to the sleepy college town of Venture, Georgia. In order for their stores to survive, Ethan and Janie will have to merge her comic book store with his traditional bookstore. The laughs are plenty as this unlikely pair find a way to get past their differences to turn the page creating a new chapter in both their lives.

Available Summer 2015